AS I LAY DYING

As I
Lay Dying

WILLIAM
FAULKNER

VINTAGE BOOKS
A Division of Random House
NEW YORK

B-- Cash finish coffin w/a broken leg?
- Land talking (167)
    Darl too (see t/land)
- won't eat in house (pa) 174
    what about Jewel (italics)

- Sawdust fer leg (187)
    2 broken legs?

- what is on
- the track
    (239)

TO

Hal Smith

Library of Congress Cataloging in Publication Data

Faulkner, William, 1897-1962.
    As I lay dying.
    I. Title.
[PZ3.F272As11] [PS3511.A86]   813'.5'2   72-8023
ISBN 0-394-70254-9

Manufactured in the United States of America
Vintage Books Edition, February 1964

Cover Photo: RAILS DANS L'OUEST, Bernard Plossu

AS I LAY DYING

Darl

Jewel and I come up from the field, following the path in single file. Although I am fifteen feet ahead of him, anyone watching us from the cottonhouse can see Jewel's frayed and broken straw hat a full head above my own.

The path runs straight as a plumb-line, worn smooth by feet and baked brick-hard by July, between the green rows of laid-by cotton, to the cottonhouse in the center of the field, where it turns and circles the cottonhouse at four soft right angles and goes on across the field again, worn so by feet in fading precision.

The cottonhouse is of rough logs, from between

which the chinking has long fallen. Square, with a broken roof set at a single pitch, it leans in empty and shimmering dilapidation in the sunlight, a single broad window in two opposite walls giving onto the approaches of the path. When we reach it I turn and follow the path which circles the house. Jewel, fifteen feet behind me, looking straight ahead, steps in a single stride through the window. Still staring straight ahead, his pale eyes like wood set into his wooden face, he crosses the floor in four strides with the rigid gravity of a cigar store Indian dressed in patched overalls and endued with life from the hips down, and steps in a single stride through the opposite window and into the path again just as I come around the corner. In single file and five feet apart and Jewel now in front, we go on up the path toward the foot of the bluff.

Tull's wagon stands beside the spring, hitched to the rail, the reins wrapped about the seat stanchion. In the wagon bed are two chairs. Jewel stops at the spring and takes the gourd from the willow branch and drinks. I pass him and mount the path, beginning to hear Cash's saw.

When I reach the top he has quit sawing. Standing in a litter of chips, he is fitting two of the boards together. Between the shadow spaces they are yellow as gold, like soft gold, bearing on their flanks in smooth undulations the marks of the adze blade: a good carpenter, Cash is. He holds the two planks on the trestle, fitted along the edges in a quarter of the finished box. He kneels and squints along the edge of them, then he lowers them and takes up the adze. A good carpenter. Addie Bundren could not want a better one,

a better box to lie in. It will give her confidence and
comfort. I go on to the house, followed by the

Chuck.   Chuck.   Chuck.

of the adze.

Cora

religious hypocrite

So I saved out the eggs and baked yesterday. The cakes turned out right well. We depend a lot on our chickens. They are good layers, what few we have left after the possums and such. Snakes too, in the summer. A snake will break up a hen-house quicker than anything. So after they were going to cost so much more than Mr Tull thought, and after I promised that the difference in the number of eggs would make it up, I had to be more careful than ever because it was on my final say-so we took them. We could have stocked cheaper chickens, but I gave my promise as Miss Lawington said when she advised me to get a good breed, because Mr Tull himself admits that a good breed of cows or hogs pays in the long run. So when we lost so many of them we couldn't afford to use the eggs ourselves, because I could not have had Mr Tull chide me when it was on my say-so we took them. So when Miss Lawington told me about the cakes I thought that I could bake them and earn enough at one time to increase the net value of the flock the equivalent of two head. And that by saving the eggs out one at a time, even the eggs wouldn't be costing anything. And that week they laid so well that I not only saved out enough eggs above what we had engaged to sell, to bake the cakes with, I had saved enough so that the flour and the sugar and the stove wood would not be costing anything. So I baked yesterday, more careful than ever I baked in my life, and the cakes turned out right well. But when we got to town this morning Miss Lawington told me the lady had changed her mind and was not going to have the party after all.

"She ought to taken those cakes anyway," Kate says.

"Well," I say, "I reckon she never had no use for them now."

"She ought to taken them," Kate says. "But those rich town ladies can change their minds. Poor folks cant."

Riches is nothing in the face of the Lord, for He can see into the heart. "Maybe I can sell them at the bazaar Saturday," I say. They turned out real well.

"You cant get two dollars a piece for them," Kate says.

"Well, it isn't like they cost me anything," I say. I saved them out and swapped a dozen of them for the sugar and flour. It isn't like the cakes cost me anything, as Mr Tull himself realises that the eggs I saved were over and beyond what we had engaged to sell, so it was like we had found the eggs or they had been given to us.

"She ought to taken those cakes when she same as gave you her word," Kate says. The Lord can see into the heart. If it is His will that some folks has different ideas of honesty from other folks, it is not my place to question His decree.

"I reckon she never had any use for them," I say. They turned out real well, too.

The quilt is drawn up to her chin, hot as it is, with only her two hands and her face outside. She is propped on the pillow, with her head raised so she can see out the window, and we can hear him every time he takes up the adze or the saw. If we were deaf we could almost watch her face and hear him, see him. Her face is wasted away so that the bones draw just under the skin in white lines. Her eyes are like two candles when you watch them gutter down into the sockets of iron candle-sticks. But the eternal and the everlasting salvation and grace is not upon her.

"They turned out real nice," I say. "But not like the cakes Addie used to bake." You can see that girl's washing and ironing in the pillow-slip, if ironed it ever was. Maybe it will reveal her blindness to her, laying there at the mercy and the ministration of four men and a tom-boy girl. "There's not a woman in this section could ever bake with Addie Bundren," I say. "First thing we know she'll be up and baking again, and then we wont have any sale for ours at all." Under the quilt she makes no more of a hump than a rail would, and the only way you can tell she is breathing is by the sound of the mattress shucks. Even the hair at her cheek does not move, even with that girl standing right over her, fanning her with the fan. While we watch she swaps the fan to the other hand without stopping it.

"Is she sleeping?" Kate whispers.

"She's just watching Cash yonder," the girl says. We can hear the saw in the board. It sounds like snoring. Eula turns on the trunk and looks out the window. Her necklace looks real nice with her red hat. You wouldn't think it only cost twenty-five cents.

"She ought to taken those cakes," Kate says.

I could have used the money real well. But it's not like they cost me anything except the baking. I can tell him that anybody is likely to make a miscue, but it's not all of them that can get out of it without loss, I can tell him. It's not everybody can eat their mistakes, I can tell him.

Someone comes through the hall. It is Darl. He does not look in as he passes the door. Eula watches him as he goes on and passes from sight again toward the back. Her hand rises and touches her beads lightly, and then her hair. When she finds me watching her, her eyes go blank.

Darl

Pa and Vernon are sitting on the back porch. Pa is tilting snuff from the lid of his snuff-box into his lower lip, holding the lip outdrawn between thumb and finger. They look around as I cross the porch and dip the gourd into the water bucket and drink.

"Where's Jewel?" pa says. When I was a boy I first learned how much better water tastes when it has set a while in a cedar bucket. Warmish-cool, with a faint taste like the hot July wind in cedar trees smells. It has to set at least six hours, and be drunk from a gourd. Water should never be drunk from metal.

And at night it is better still. I used to lie on the pallet in the hall, waiting until I could hear them all asleep, so I could get up and go back to the bucket. It would be black, the shelf black, the still surface of the water a round orifice in nothingness, where before I stirred it awake with the dipper I could see maybe a star or two in the bucket, and maybe in the dipper a star or two before I drank. After that I was bigger, older. Then I would wait until they all went to sleep so I could lie with my shirt-tail up, hearing them asleep, feeling myself without touching myself, feeling the cool silence blowing upon my parts and wondering if Cash was yonder in the darkness doing it too, had been doing it perhaps for the last two years before I could have wanted to or could have.

Pa's feet are badly splayed, his toes cramped and bent and warped, with no toenail at all on his little toes, from working so hard in the wet in homemade shoes when he was a boy. Beside his chair his brogans sit. They look as though they had been hacked with a blunt axe out of pig-iron. Vernon has been to town. I have never seen him go to town in overalls. His wife, they say. She taught school too, once.

I fling the dipper dregs to the ground and wipe my mouth on my sleeve. It is going to rain before morning. Maybe before dark. "Down to the barn," I say. "Harnessing the team."

Down there fooling with that horse. He will go on through the barn, into the pasture. The horse will not be in sight: he is up there among the pine seedlings, in the cool. Jewel whistles, once and shrill. The horse snorts, then Jewel sees him, glinting for a gaudy instant among the blue shadows. Jewel whistles again; the horse comes dropping down the slope, stiff-legged, his ears cocking and flicking, his mis-matched eyes rolling, and fetches up twenty feet away, broadside on, watching Jewel over his shoulder in an attitude kittenish and alert.

"Come here, sir," Jewel says. He moves. Moving that quick his coat, bunching, tongues swirling like so many flames. With tossing mane and tail and rolling eye the horse makes another short curvetting rush and stops again, feet bunched, watching Jewel. Jewel walks steadily toward him, his hands at his sides. Save for Jewel's legs they are like two figures carved for a tableau savage in the sun.

When Jewel can almost touch him, the horse stands on his hind legs and slashes down at Jewel. Then Jewel is enclosed by a glittering maze of hooves as by an illusion of wings; among them, beneath the upreared chest, he moves with the flashing limberness of a snake. For an instant before the jerk comes onto his arms he sees his whole body earth-free, horizontal, whipping snake-limber, until he finds the horse's nostrils and touches earth again. Then they are rigid, motionless, terrific, the horse back-thrust on stiffened, quivering legs, with lowered head; Jewel with dug heels, shutting off the horse's wind with one hand, with the other patting the horse's neck in short strokes myriad and caressing, cursing the horse with obscene ferocity.

They stand in rigid terrific hiatus, the horse trembling and groaning. Then Jewel is on the horse's back. He flows upward in a stooping swirl like the lash of a whip, his body in midair shaped to the horse. For another moment the horse stands spraddled, with lowered head, before it bursts into motion. They descend the hill in a series of spine-jolting jumps, Jewel high, leech-like on the withers, to the fence where the horse bunches to a scuttering halt again.

"Well," Jewel says, "you can quit now, if you got a-plenty."

Inside the barn Jewel slides running to the ground before the horse stops. The horse enters the stall, Jewel following. Without looking back the horse kicks at him, slamming a single hoof into the wall with a pistol-like report. Jewel kicks him in the stomach; the horse arches his neck back, crop-toothed; Jewel strikes him across the face with his fist and slides on to the trough and mounts upon it. Clinging to the hay-rack he lowers his head and peers out across the stall tops and through the doorway. The path is empty; from here he cannot even hear Cash sawing. He reaches up and drags down hay in hurried armsful and crams it into the rack.

"Eat," he says. "Get the goddamn stuff out of sight while you got a chance, you pussel-gutted bastard. You sweet son of a bitch," he says.

[handwritten annotation:] HORSE IS A SURROGATE FOR JEWEL'S MOTHER. HATE-LOVE RELATIONSHIP

Jewel

It's because he stays out there, right under the window, hammering and sawing on that goddamn box. Where she's got to see him. Where every breath she draws is full of his knocking and sawing where she can see him saying See. See what a good one I am making for you. I told him to go somewhere else. I said Good God do you want to see her in it. It's like when he was a little boy and she says if she had some fertilizer she would try to raise some flowers and he taken the bread pan and brought it back from the barn full of dung.

And now them others sitting there, like buzzards. Waiting, fanning themselves. Because I said If you wouldn't keep on sawing and nailing at it until a man *thinking of mother in the ground*

Everything they do is wrong

cant sleep even and her hands laying on the quilt like two of them roots dug up and tried to wash and you couldn't get them clean. I can see the fan and Dewey Dell's arm. I said if you'd just let her alone. Sawing and knocking, and keeping the air always moving so fast on her face that when you're tired you cant breathe it, and that goddamn adze going One lick less. One lick less. One lick less until everybody that passes in the road will have to stop and see it and say what a fine carpenter he is. If it had just been me when Cash fell off of that church and if it had just been me when pa laid sick with that load of wood fell on him, it would not be happening with every bastard in the county coming in to stare at her because if there is a God what the hell is He for. It would just be me and her on a high hill and me rolling the rocks down the hill at their faces, picking them up and throwing them down the hill faces and teeth and all by God until she was quiet and not that goddamn adze going One lick less. One lick less and we could be quiet.

Dad
CHICK CHICK chuck

*He wouldn't demand work from his mother.
—Or would he probably demand more*

Jewel has bad view of everyone.

Mother fixation.

Enemies w/ everyone bc of it

Cash would say Jewel needed the attention

Darl

We watch him come around the corner and mount the steps. He does not look at us. "You ready?" he says.

"If you're hitched up," I say. I say "Wait." He stops, looking at pa. Vernon spits, without moving. He spits with decorous and deliberate precision into the pocked dust below the porch. Pa rubs his hands slowly on his knees. He is gazing out beyond the crest of the bluff, out across the land. Jewel watches him a moment, then he goes on to the pail and drinks again.

"I mislike undecision as much as ere a man," pa says.

"It means three dollars," I say. The shirt across pa's hump is faded lighter than the rest of it. There is no sweat stain on his shirt. I have never seen a sweat stain on his shirt. He was sick once from working in the sun when he was twenty-two years old, and he tells people that if he ever sweats, he will die. I suppose he believes it.

"But if she dont last until you get back," he says. "She will be disappointed."

Vernon spits into the dust. But it will rain before morning.

"She's counted on it," pa says. "She'll want to start right away. I know her. I promised her I'd keep the team here and ready, and she's counting on it."

"We'll need that three dollars then, sure," I say. He gazes out over the land, rubbing his hands on his knees. Since he lost his teeth his mouth collapses in slow repetition when he dips. The stubble gives his lower face that appearance that old dogs have. "You'd better make up your mind soon, so we can get there and get a load on before dark," I say.

"Ma aint that sick," Jewel says. "Shut up, Darl."

"That's right," Vernon says. "She seems more like herself today than she has in a week. Time you and Jewel get back, she'll be setting up."

"You ought to know," Jewel says. "You been here often enough looking at her. You or your folks." Vernon looks at him. Jewel's eyes look like pale wood in his high-blooded face. He is a head taller than any of the rest of us, always was. I told them that's why ma always whipped him and petted him more. Because he was peakling around the house more. That's why she named him Jewel I told them.

"Shut up, Jewel," pa says, but as though he is not listening much. He gazes out across the land, rubbing his knees.

"You could borrow the loan of Vernon's team and

we could catch up with you," I say. "If she didn't wait
for us."

"Ah, shut your goddamn mouth," Jewel says.

"She'll want to go in ourn," pa says. He rubs his
knees. "Dont ere a man mislike it more."

"It's laying there, watching Cash whittle on that
damn . . ." Jewel says. He says it harshly, savagely,
but he does not say the word. Like a little boy in the
dark to flail his courage and suddenly aghast into silence by his own noise.

"She wanted that like she wants to go in our own
wagon," pa says. "She'll rest easier for knowing it's a
good one, and private. She was ever a private woman.
You know it well."

"Then let it be private," Jewel says. "But how the
hell can you expect it to be—" he looks at the back of
pa's head, his eyes like pale wooden eyes.

"Sho," Vernon says, "she'll hold on till it's finished.
She'll hold on till everything's ready, till her own good
time. And with the roads like they are now, it wont
take you no time to get her to town."

"It's fixing up to rain," pa says. "I am a luckless man.
I have ever been." He rubs his hands on his knees.
"It's that durn doctor, liable to come at any time. I
couldn't get word to him till so late. If he was to come
tomorrow and tell her the time was nigh, she wouldn't
wait. I know her. Wagon or no wagon, she wouldn't
wait. Then she'd be upset, and I wouldn't upset her
for the living world. With that family burying-ground
in Jefferson and them of her blood waiting for her
there, she'll be impatient. I promised my word me and
the boys would get her there quick as mules could
walk it, so she could rest quiet." He rubs his hands on
his knees. "No man ever misliked it more."

"If everybody wasn't burning hell to get her there," Jewel says in that harsh, savage voice. "With Cash all day long right under the window, hammering and sawing at that—"

"It was her wish," pa says. "You got no affection nor gentleness for her. You never had. We would be beholden to no man," he says, "me and her. We have never yet been, and she will rest quieter for knowing it and that it was her own blood sawed out the boards and drove the nails. She was ever one to clean up after herself."

"It means three dollars," I say. "Do you want us to go, or not?" Pa rubs his knees. "We'll be back by tomorrow sundown."

"Well . . ." pa says. He looks out over the land, awry-haired, mouthing the snuff slowly against his gums.

"Come on," Jewel says. He goes down the steps. Vernon spits neatly into the dust.

"By sundown, now," pa says. "I would not keep her waiting."

Jewel glances back, then he goes on around the house. I enter the hall, hearing the voices before I reach the door. Tilting a little down the hill, as our house does, a breeze draws through the hall all the time, upslanting. A feather dropped near the front door will rise and brush along the ceiling, slanting backward, until it reaches the down-turning current at the back door: so with voices. As you enter the hall, they sound as though they were speaking out of the air about your head.

Cora 4

It was the sweetest thing I ever saw. It was like he knew he would never see her again, that Anse Bundren was driving him from his mother's death bed, never to see her in this world again. I always said Darl was different from those others. I always said he was the only one of them that had his mother's nature, had any natural affection. Not that Jewel, the one she labored so to bear and coddled and petted so and him flinging into tantrums or sulking spells, inventing devilment to devil her until I would have frailed him time and time. Not him to come and tell her goodbye. Not him to miss a chance to make that extra three dollars at the price of his mother's goodbye kiss. A Bundren through and through, loving no-body, caring for nothing except how to get something with the least amount of work. Mr Tull says Darl asked them to wait. He said Darl almost begged them on his knees not to force him to leave her in her con-dition. But nothing would do but Anse and Jewel must make that three dollars. Nobody that knows Anse could have expected different, but to think of that boy, that Jewel, selling all those years of self-denial and down-right partiality—they couldn't fool me: Mr Tull says Mrs Bundren liked Jewel the least of all, but I knew better. I knew she was partial to him, to the same quality in him that let her put up with Anse Bundren when Mr Tull said she ought to poisoned him—for three dollars, denying his dying mother the goodbye kiss.

Why, for the last three weeks I have been coming over every time I could, coming sometimes when I shouldn't have, neglecting my own family and duties so that somebody would be with her in her last mo-ments and she would not have to face the Great Un-known without one familiar face to give her courage. Not that I deserve credit for it: I will expect the same for myself. But thank God it will be the faces of my loved kin, my blood and flesh, for in my husband and children I have been more blessed than most, trials though they have been at times.

She lived, a lonely woman, lonely with her pride, trying to make folks believe different, hiding the fact that they just suffered her, because she was not cold in the coffin before they were carting her forty miles away to bury her, flouting the will of God to do it. Refusing to let her lie in the same earth with those Bundrens.

CORA THINKS THE FAMILY
DOESN'T LOVE ADDIE.
SHE SEES DARL IN A GOOD LIGHT

"But she wanted to go," Mr Tull said. "It was her own wish to lie among her own people."

"Then why didn't she go alive?" I said. "Not one of them would have stopped her, with even that little one almost old enough now to be selfish and stone-hearted like the rest of them."

"It was her own wish," Mr Tull said. "I heard Anse say it was."

"And you would believe Anse, of course," I said. "A man like you would. Dont tell me."

"I'd believe him about something he couldn't expect to make anything off of me by not telling," Mr Tull said.

"Dont tell me," I said. "A woman's place is with her husband and children, alive or dead. Would you expect me to want to go back to Alabama and leave you and the girls when my time comes, that I left of my own will to cast my lot with yours for better and worse, until death and after?"

"Well, folks are different," he said.

I should hope so. I have tried to live right in the sight of God and man, for the honor and comfort of my Christian husband and the love and respect of my Christian children. So that when I lay me down in the consciousness of my duty and reward I will be surrounded by loving faces, carrying the farewell kiss of each of my loved ones into my reward. Not like Addie Bundren dying alone, hiding her pride and her broken heart. Glad to go. Lying there with her head propped up so she could watch Cash building the coffin, having to watch him so he would not skimp on it, like as not, with those men not worrying about anything except if there was time to earn another three dollars before the rain come and the river got too high to get across it. Like as not, if they hadn't decided to make that last load, they would have loaded her into the wagon on a quilt and crossed the river first and then stopped and give her time to die what Christian death they would let her.

Except Darl. It was the sweetest thing I ever saw. Sometimes I lose faith in human nature for a time; I am assailed by doubt. But always the Lord restores my faith and reveals to me His bounteous love for His creatures. Not Jewel, the one she had always cherished, not him. He was after that three extra dollars. It was Darl, the one that folks say is queer, lazy, pottering about the place no better than Anse, with Cash a good carpenter and always more building than he can get around to, and Jewel always doing something that made him some money or got him talked about, and that near-naked girl always standing over Addie with a fan so that every time a body tried to talk to her and cheer her up, would answer for her right quick, like she was trying to keep anybody from coming near her at all.

It was Darl. He come to the door and stood there, looking at his dying mother. He just looked at her, and I felt the bounteous love of the Lord again and His mercy. I saw that with Jewel she had just been pretending, but that it was between her and Darl that the understanding and the true love was. He just looked at her, not even coming in where she could see him and get upset, knowing that Anse was driving him away and he would never see her again. He said nothing, just looking at her.

"What you want, Darl?" Dewey Dell said, not

stopping the fan, speaking up quick, keeping even him from her. He didn't answer. He just stood and looked at his dying mother, his heart too full for words.

Dewey Dell

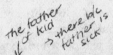

The first time me and Lafe picked on down the row.
Pa dassent sweat because he will catch his death from
the sickness so everybody that comes to help us. And
Jewel dont care about anything he is not kin to us in
caring, not care-kin. And Cash like sawing the long
hot sad yellow days up into planks and nailing them
to something. And pa thinks because neighbors will
always treat one another that way because he has always been too busy letting neighbors do for him to
find out. And I did not think that Darl would, that sits
at the supper table with his eyes gone further than
the food and the lamp, full of the land dug out of his

skull and the holes filled with distance beyond the land.

We picked on down the row, the woods getting closer and closer and the secret shade, picking on into the secret shade with my sack and Lafe's sack. Because I said will I or wont I when the sack was half full because I said if the sack is full when we get to the woods it wont be me. I said if it dont mean for me to do it the sack will not be full and I will turn up the next row but if the sack is full, I cannot help it. It will be that I had to do it all the time and I cannot help it. And we picked on toward the secret shade and our eyes would drown together touching on his hands and my hands and I didn't say anything. I said "What are you doing?" and he said "I am picking into your sack." And so it was full when we came to the end of the row and I could not help it.

And so it was because I could not help it. It was then, and then I saw Darl and he knew. He said he knew without the words like he told me that ma is going to die without words, and I knew he knew because if he had said he knew with the words I would not have believed that he had been there and saw us. But he said he did know and I said "Are you going to tell pa are you going to kill him?" without the words I said it and he said "Why?" without the words. And that's why I can talk to him with knowing with hating because he knows.

He stands in the door, looking at her.

"What you want, Darl?" I say.

"She is going to die," he says. And old turkey-buzzard Tull coming to watch her die but I can fool them.

Darl insults Caa.

"When is she going to die?" I say.
"Before we get back," he says.
"Then why are you taking Jewel?" I say.
"I want him to help me load," he says.

Tull 8

Anse keeps on rubbing his knees. His overalls are faded; on one knee a serge patch cut out of a pair of Sunday pants, wore iron-slick. "No man mislikes it more than me," he says.

"A fellow's got to guess ahead now and then," I say. "But, come long and short, it wont be no harm done neither way."

"She'll want to get started right off," he says. "It's far enough to Jefferson at best."

"But the roads is good now," I say. It's fixing to rain tonight, too. His folks buries at New Hope, too, not three miles away. But it's just like him to marry a woman born a day's hard ride away and have her die on him.

He looks out over the land, rubbing his knees. "No man so mislikes it," he says.

"They'll get back in plenty of time," I say. "I wouldn't worry none."

"It means three dollars," he says.

"Might be it wont be no need for them to rush back, noways," I say. "I hope it."

"She's a-going," he says. "Her mind is set on it."

It's a hard life on women, for a fact. Some women. I mind my mammy lived to be seventy and more. Worked every day, rain or shine; never a sick day since her last chap was born until one day she kind of looked around her and then she went and taken that lace-trimmed night gown she had had forty-five years and never wore out of the chest and put it on and laid down on the bed and pulled the covers up and shut her eyes. "You all will have to look out for pa the best you can," she said. "I'm tired."

Anse rubs his hands on his knees. "The Lord giveth," he says. We can hear Cash a-hammering and sawing beyond the corner.

It's true. Never a truer breath was ever breathed. "The Lord giveth," I say.

That boy comes up the hill. He is carrying a fish nigh long as he is. He slings it to the ground and grunts "Hah" and spits over his shoulder like a man. Durn nigh long as he is.

"What's that?" I say. "A hog? Where'd you get it?"

"Down to the bridge," he says. He turns it over, the under side caked over with dust where it is wet, the eye coated over, humped under the dirt.

"Are you aiming to leave it laying there?" Anse says.

"I aim to show it to ma," Vardaman says. He looks toward the door. We can hear the talking, coming out on the draft. Cash too, knocking and hammering at the boards. "There's company in there," he says.

"Just my folks," I say. "They'd enjoy to see it too."

He says nothing, watching the door. Then he looks down at the fish laying in the dust. He turns it over with his foot and prods at the eye-bump with his toe, gouging at it. Anse is looking out over the land. Vardaman looks at Anse's face, then at the door. He turns, going toward the corner of the house, when Anse calls him without looking around.

"You clean that fish," Anse says.

Vardaman stops. "Why cant Dewey Dell clean it?" he says.

"You clean that fish," Anse says.

"Aw, pa," Vardaman says.

"You clean it," Anse says. He dont look around. Vardaman comes back and picks up the fish. It slides out of his hands, smearing wet dirt onto him, and flops down, dirtying itself again, gapmouthed, goggle-eyed, hiding into the dust like it was ashamed of being dead, like it was in a hurry to get back hid again. Vardaman cusses it. He cusses it like a grown man, standing a-straddle of it. Anse dont look around. Vardaman picks it up again. He goes on around the house, toting it in both arms like a armful of wood, it overlapping him on both ends, head and tail. Durn nigh big as he is.

Anse's wrists dangle out of his sleeves: I never see him with a shirt on that looked like it was his in all my life. They all looked like Jewel might have give him his old ones. Not Jewel, though. He's long-armed, even if he is spindling. Except for the lack of sweat. You could tell they aint been nobody else's but Anse's that way without no mistake. His eyes look like pieces of burnt-out cinder fixed in his face, looking out over the land.

When the shadow touches the steps he says "It's five oclock."

Just as I get up Cora comes to the door and says it's time to get on. Anse reaches for his shoes. "Now, Mr Bundren," Cora says, "dont you get up now." He puts his shoes on, stomping into them, like he does everything, like he is hoping all the time he really cant do it and can quit trying to. When we go up the hall we can hear them clumping on the floor like they was iron shoes. He comes toward the door where she is, blinking his eyes, kind of looking ahead of hisself before he sees, like he is hoping to find her setting up, in a chair maybe or maybe sweeping, and looks into the door in that surprised way like he looks in and finds her still in bed every time and Dewey Dell still a-fanning her with the fan. He stands there, like he dont aim to move again nor nothing else.

"Well, I reckon we better get on," Cora says. "I got to feed the chickens." It's fixing to rain, too. Clouds like that dont lie, and the cotton making every day the Lord sends. That'll be something else for him. Cash is still trimming at the boards. "If there's ere a thing we can do," Cora says.

"Anse'll let us know," I say.

Anse dont look at us. He looks around, blinking, in that surprised way, like he had wore hisself down being surprised and was even surprised at that. If Cash just works that careful on my barn.

"I told Anse it likely wont be no need," I say. "I so hope it."

"Her mind is set on it," he says. "I reckon she's bound to go."

"It comes to all of us," Cora says. "Let the Lord comfort you."

"About that corn," I say. I tell him again I will help him out if he gets into a tight, with her sick and all. Like most folks around here, I done holp him so much already I cant quit now.

"I aimed to get to it today," he says. "Seems like I cant get my mind on nothing."

"Maybe she'll hold out till you are laid-by," I say.

"If God wills it," he says.

"Let Him comfort you," Cora says.

If Cash just works that careful on my barn. He looks up when we pass. "Dont reckon I'll get to you this week," he says.

" 'Taint no rush," I say. "Whenever you get around to it."

We get into the wagon. Cora sets the cake box on her lap. It's fixing to rain, sho.

"I dont know what he'll do," Cora says. "I just dont know."

"Poor Anse," I say. "She kept him at work for thirty-odd years. I reckon she is tired."

"And I reckon she'll be behind him for thirty years more," Kate says. "Or if it aint her, he'll get another one before cotton-picking."

"I reckon Cash and Darl can get married now," Eula says.

"That poor boy," Cora says. "The poor little tyke."

"What about Jewel?" Kate says.

"He can, too," Eula says.

"Hmph," Kate says. "I reckon he will. I reckon so. I reckon there's more gals than one around here that dont want to see Jewel tied down. Well, they needn't to worry."

"Why, Kate!" Cora says. The wagon begins to rattle. "The poor little tyke," Cora says.

It's fixing to rain this night. Yes, sir. A rattling wagon is mighty dry weather, for a Birdsell. But that'll be cured. It will for a fact.

"She ought to taken them cakes after she said she would," Kate says.

Anse

Durn that road. And it fixing to rain, too. I can stand here and same as see it with second-sight, a-shutting down behind them like a wall, shutting down betwixt them and my given promise. I do the best I can, much as I can get my mind on anything, but durn them boys.

A-laying there, right up to my door, where every bad luck that comes and goes is bound to find it. I told Addie it want any luck living on a road when it come by here, and she said, for the world like a woman, "Get up and move, then." But I told her it want no luck in it, because the Lord put roads for travelling: why He laid them down flat on the earth. When He aims for something to be always a-moving,

He makes it longways, like a road or a horse or a
wagon, but when He aims for something to stay put,
He makes it up-and-down ways, like a tree or a man.
And so he never aimed for folks to live on a road,
because which gets there first, I says, the road or the
house? Did you ever know Him to set a road down
by a house? I says. No you never, I says, because it's
always men cant rest till they gets the house set where
everybody that passes in a wagon can spit in the doorway, keeping the folks restless and wanting to get up
and go somewheres else when He aimed for them to
stay put like a tree or a stand of corn. Because if He'd
a aimed for man to be always a-moving and going
somewheres else, wouldn't He a put him longways
on his belly, like a snake? It stands to reason He
would.

Putting it where every bad luck prowling can find
it and come straight to my door, charging me taxes on
top of it. Making me pay for Cash having to get them
carpenter notions when if it hadn't been no road come
there, he wouldn't a got them; falling off of churches
and lifting no hand in six months and me and Addie
slaving and a-slaving, when there's plenty of sawing
on this place he could do if he's got to saw.

And Darl too. Talking me out of him, durn them.
It aint that I am afraid of work; I always is fed me
and mine and kept a roof above us: it's that they
would short-hand me just because he tends to his own
business, just because he's got his eyes full of the
land all the time. I says to them, he was all right at
first, with his eyes full of the land, because the land
laid up-and-down ways then; it wasn't till that ere
road come and switched the land around longways
and his eyes still full of the land, that they begun to

threaten me out of him, trying to short-hand me with the law.

Making me pay for it. She was well and hale as ere a woman ever were, except for that road. Just laying down, resting herself in her own bed, asking naught of none. "Are you sick, Addie?" I said.

"I am not sick," she said.

"You lay you down and rest you," I said. "I knowed you are not sick. You're just tired. You lay you down and rest."

"I am not sick," she said. "I will get up."

"Lay still and rest," I said. "You are just tired. You can get up tomorrow." And she was laying there, well and hale as ere a woman ever were, except for that road.

"I never sent for you," I said. "I take you to witness I never sent for you."

"I know you didn't," Peabody said. "I bound that. Where is she?"

"She's a-laying down," I said. "She's just a little tired, but she'll—"

"Get outen here, Anse," he said. "Go set on the porch a while."

And now I got to pay for it, me without a tooth in my head, hoping to get ahead enough so I could get my mouth fixed where I could eat God's own victuals as a man should, and her hale and well as ere a woman in the land until that day. Got to pay for being put to the need of that three dollars. Got to pay for the way for them boys to have to go away to earn it. And now I can see same as second sight the rain shutting down betwixt us, a-coming up that road like a durn man, like it want ere a other house to rain on in all the living land.

I have heard men cuss their luck, and right, for they were sinful men. But I do not say it's a curse on me, because I have done no wrong to be cussed by. I am not religious, I reckon. But peace is my heart: I know it is. I have done things but neither better nor worse than them that pretend otherlike, and I know that Old Marster will care for me as for ere a sparrow that falls. But it seems hard that a man in his need could be so flouted by a road.

Vardaman comes around the house, bloody as a hog to his knees, and that ere fish chopped up with the axe like as not, or maybe throwed away for him to lie about the dogs et it. Well, I reckon I aint no call to expect no more of him than of his man-growed brothers. He comes along, watching the house, quiet, and sits on the steps. "Whew," he says, "I'm pure tired."

"Go wash them hands," I say. But couldn't no woman strove harder than Addie to make them right, man and boy: I'll say that for her.

"It was full of blood and guts as a hog," he says. But I just cant seem to get no heart into anything, with this here weather sapping me, too. "Pa," he says, "is ma sick some more?"

"Go wash them hands," I say. But I just cant seem to get no heart into it.

Darl

He has been to town this week: the back of his neck is trimmed close, with a white line between hair and sunburn like a joint of white bone. He has not once looked back.

"Jewel," I say. Back running, tunnelled between the two sets of bobbing mule ears, the road vanishes beneath the wagon as though it were a ribbon and the front axle were a spool. "Do you know she is going to die, Jewel?"

It takes two people to make you, and one people to die. That's how the world is going to end.

I said to Dewey Dell: "You want her to die so you can get to town: is that it?" She wouldn't say what we both knew. "The reason you will not say it is, when you say it, even to yourself, you will know it is true: is that it? But you know it is true now. I can almost tell you the day when you knew it is true. Why wont you say it, even to yourself?" She will not say it. She just keeps on saying Are you going to tell pa? Are you going to kill him? "You cannot believe it is true because you cannot believe that Dewey Dell, Dewey Dell Bundren, could have such bad luck: is that it?"

The sun, an hour above the horizon, is poised like a bloody egg upon a crest of thunderheads; the light has turned copper: in the eye portentous, in the nose sulphurous, smelling of lightning. When Peabody comes, they will have to use the rope. He has pussel-gutted himself eating cold greens. With the rope they will haul him up the path, balloon-like up the sulphurous air.

"Jewel," I say, "do you know that Addie Bundren is going to die? Addie Bundren is going to die?"

Peabody

When Anse finally sent for me of his own accord, I said "He has wore her out at last." And I said a damn good thing, and at first I would not go because there might be something I could do and I would have to haul her back, by God. I thought maybe they have the same sort of fool ethics in heaven they have in the Medical College and that it was maybe Vernon Tull sending for me again, getting me there in the nick of time, as Vernon always does things, getting the most for Anse's money like he does for his own. But when it got far enough into the day for me to read weather sign I knew it couldn't have been anybody but Anse that sent. I knew that nobody but a luckless man could ever need a doctor in the face of a cyclone. And I knew that if it had finally occurred to Anse himself that he needed one, it was already too late.

When I reach the spring and get down and hitch the team, the sun has gone down behind a bank of black cloud like a topheavy mountain range, like a load of cinders dumped over there, and there is no wind. I could hear Cash sawing for a mile before I got there. Anse is standing at the top of the bluff above the path.

"Where's the horse?" I say.

"Jewel's taken and gone," he says. "Cant nobody else ketch hit. You'll have to walk up, I reckon."

"Me, walk up, weighing two hundred and twenty-five pounds?" I say. "Walk up that durn wall?" He stands there beside a tree. Too bad the Lord made the mistake of giving trees roots and giving the Anse Bundrens He makes feet and legs. If He'd just swapped them, there wouldn't ever be a worry about this country being deforested someday. Or any other country. "What do you aim for me to do?" I say. "Stay here and get blowed clean out of the county when that cloud breaks?" Even with the horse it would take me fifteen minutes to ride up across the pasture to the top of the ridge and reach the house. The path looks like a crooked limb blown against the bluff. Anse has not been in town in twelve years. And how his mother ever got up there to bear him, he being his mother's son.

"Vardaman's gittin the rope," he says.

After a while Vardaman appears with the plowline. He gives the end of it to Anse and comes down the path, uncoiling it.

"You hold it tight," I say. "I done already wrote this visit onto my books, so I'm going to charge you just the same, whether I get there or not."

"I got hit," Anse says. "You kin come on up."

I'll be damned if I can see why I dont quit. A man seventy years old, weighing two hundred and odd pounds, being hauled up and down a damn mountain on a rope. I reckon it's because I must reach the fifty thousand dollar mark of dead accounts on my books before I can quit. "What the hell does your wife mean," I say, "taking sick on top of a durn mountain?"

"I'm right sorry," he says. He let the rope go, just dropped it, and he has turned toward the house. There is a little daylight up here still, of the color of sulphur matches. The boards look like strips of sulphur. Cash does not look back. Vernon Tull says he brings each board up to the window for her to see it and say it is all right. The boy overtakes us. Anse looks back at him. "Wher's the rope?" he says.

"It's where you left it," I say. "But never you mind that rope. I got to get back down that bluff. I dont aim for that storm to catch me up here. I'd blow too durn far once I got started."

The girl is standing by the bed, fanning her. When we enter she turns her head and looks at us. She has been dead these ten days. I suppose it's having been a part of Anse for so long that she cannot even make that change, if change it be. I can remember how when I was young I believed death to be a phenomenon of the body; now I know it to be merely a function of the mind—and that of the minds of the ones who suffer the bereavement. The nihilists say it is the end; the fundamentalists, the beginning; when in reality it is no more than a single tenant or family moving out of a tenement or a town.

She looks at us. Only her eyes seem to move. It's like they touch us, not with sight or sense, but like the stream from a hose touches you, the stream at the instant of impact as dissociated from the nozzle as though it had never been there. She does not look at Anse at all. She looks at me, then at the boy. Beneath the quilt she is no more than a bundle of rotten sticks.

"Well, Miss Addie," I say. The girl does not stop the fan. "How are you, sister?" I say. Her head lies gaunt on the pillow, looking at the boy. "You picked out a fine time to get me out here and bring up a storm." Then I send Anse and the boy out. She watches the boy as he leaves the room. She has not moved save her eyes.

He and Anse are on the porch when I come out, the boy sitting on the steps, Anse standing by a post, not even leaning against it, his arms dangling, the hair pushed and matted up on his head like a dipped rooster. He turns his head, blinking at me.

"Why didn't you send for me sooner?" I say.

"Hit was jest one thing and then another," he says. "That ere corn me and the boys was aimin to git up with, and Dewey Dell a-takin good keer of her, and folks comin in, a-offerin to help and sich, till I jest thought . . ."

"Damn the money," I say. "Did you ever hear of me worrying a fellow before he was ready to pay?"

"Hit aint begrudgin the money," he says. "I jest kept a-thinkin . . . She's goin, is she?" The durn little tyke *Vard.* is sitting on the top step, looking smaller than ever in the sulphur-colored light. That's the one trouble with this country: everything, weather, all, hangs on too long. Like our rivers, our land: opaque, slow, violent; shaping and creating the life of man in its implacable and brooding image. "I knowed hit," Anse says. "All the while I made sho. Her mind is sot on hit."

"And a damn good thing, too," I say. "With a trifling—" He sits on the top step, small, motionless in faded overalls. When I came out he looked up at me, then at Anse. But now he has stopped looking at us. He just sits there.

"Have you told her yit?" Anse says.

"What for?" I say. "What the devil for?"

"She'll know hit. I knowed that when she see you she would know hit, same as writing. You wouldn't need to tell her. Her mind—"

Behind us the girl says, "<u>Paw</u>." I look at her, at her face.

"You better go quick," I say.

When we enter the room she is watching the door. She looks at me. Her eyes look like lamps blaring up just before the oil is gone. "She wants you to go out," the girl says.

"Now, Addie," Anse says, "when he come all the way from Jefferson to git you well?" She watches me: I can feel her eyes. It's like she was shoving at me with them. I have seen it before in women. Seen them drive from the room them coming with sympathy and pity, with actual help, and clinging to some trifling animal to whom they never were more than packhorses. That's what they mean by the love that passeth understanding: that pride, that furious desire to hide that abject nakedness which we bring here with us, carry with us into operating rooms, carry stubbornly and furiously with us into the earth again. I leave the room. Beyond the porch Cash's saw snores steadily into the board. A minute later she calls his name, her voice harsh and strong.

"Cash," she says; "you, Cash!"

Darl

Pa stands beside the bed. From behind his leg Vardaman peers, with his round head and his eyes round and his mouth beginning to open. She looks at pa; all her failing life appears to drain into her eyes, urgent, irremediable. "It's Jewel she wants," Dewey Dell says.

"Why, Addie," pa says, "him and Darl went to make one more load. They thought there was time. That you would wait for them, and that three dollars and all . . ." He stoops laying his hand on hers. For a while yet she looks at him, without reproach, without anything at all, as if her eyes alone are listening to the irrevocable cessation of his voice. Then she raises

herself, who has not moved in ten days. Dewey Dell
leans down, trying to press her back.

"Ma," she says; "ma."

She is looking out the window, at Cash stooping
steadily at the board in the failing light, laboring on
toward darkness and into it as though the stroking of
the saw illumined its own motion, board and saw
engendered.

"You, Cash," she shouts, her voice harsh, strong,
and unimpaired. "You, Cash!"

He looks up at the gaunt face framed by the window in the twilight. It is a composite picture of all
time since he was a child. He drops the saw and lifts
the board for her to see, watching the window in
which the face has not moved. He drags a second
plank into position and slants the two of them into
their final juxtaposition, gesturing toward the ones
yet on the ground, shaping with his empty hand in
pantomime the finished box. For a while still she looks
down at him from the composite picture, neither with
censure nor approbation. Then the face disappears.

She lies back and turns her head without so much
as glancing at pa. She looks at Vardaman; her eyes,
the life in them, rushing suddenly upon them; the two
flames glare up for a steady instant. Then they go out
as though someone had leaned down and blown upon
them.

"Ma," Dewey Dell says; "ma!" Leaning above the
bed, her hands lifted a little, the fan still moving like
it has for ten days, she begins to keen. Her voice is
strong, young, tremulous and clear, rapt with its own
timbre and volume, the fan still moving steadily up
and down, whispering the useless air. Then she flings

herself across Addie Bundren's knees, clutching her, shaking her with the furious strength of the young before sprawling suddenly across the handful of rotten bones that Addie Bundren left, jarring the whole bed into a chattering sibilance of mattress shucks, her arms outflung and the fan in one hand still beating with expiring breath into the quilt.

From behind pa's leg Vardaman peers, his mouth full open and all color draining from his face into his mouth, as though he has by some means fleshed his own teeth in himself, sucking. He begins to move slowly backward from the bed, his eyes round, his pale face fading into the dusk like a piece of paper pasted on a failing wall, and so out of the door.

Pa leans above the bed in the twilight, his humped silhouette partaking of that owl-like quality of awry-feathered, disgruntled outrage within which lurks a wisdom too profound or too inert for even thought.

"Durn them boys," he says.

Jewel, I say. Overhead the day drives level and gray, hiding the sun by a flight of gray spears. In the rain the mules smoke a little, splashed yellow with mud, the off one clinging in sliding lunges to the side of the road above the ditch. The tilted lumber gleams dull yellow, water-soaked and heavy as lead, tilted at a steep angle into the ditch above the broken wheel; about the shattered spokes and about Jewel's ankles a runnel of yellow neither water nor earth swirls, curving with the yellow road neither of earth nor water, down the hill dissolving into a streaming mass of dark green neither of earth nor sky. Jewel, I say

Cash comes to the door, carrying the saw. Pa stands beside the bed, humped, his arms dangling. He turns

his head, his shabby profile, his chin collapsing slowly
as he works the snuff against his gums.

"She's gone," Cash says.

"She taken and left us," pa says. Cash does not
look at him. "How nigh are you done?" pa says. Cash
does not answer. He enters, carrying the saw. "I
reckon you better get at it," pa says. "You'll have to
do the best you can, with them boys gone off that-a-
way." Cash looks down at her face. He is not listening
to pa at all. He does not approach the bed. He stops
in the middle of the floor, the saw against his leg,
his sweating arms powdered lightly with sawdust, his
face composed. "If you get in a tight, maybe some
of them'll get here tomorrow and help you," pa says.
"Vernon could." Cash is not listening. He is looking
down at her peaceful, rigid face fading into the dusk
as though darkness were a precursor of the ultimate
earth, until at last the face seems to float detached
upon it, lightly as the reflection of a dead leaf. "There
is Christians enough to help you," pa says. Cash is not
listening. After a while he turns without looking at pa
and leaves the room. Then the saw begins to snore
again. "They will help us in our sorrow," pa says.

The sound of the saw is steady, competent, unhur-
ried, stirring the dying light so that at each stroke
her face seems to wake a little into an expression of
listening and of waiting, as though she were counting
the strokes. Pa looks down at the face, at the black
sprawl of Dewey Dell's hair, the outflung arms, the
clutched fan now motionless on the sagging quilt. "I
reckon you better get supper on," he says.

Dewey Dell does not move.

"Git up, now, and put supper on," pa says. "We

got to keep our strength up. I reckon Doctor Peabody's right hungry, coming all this way. And Cash'll need to eat quick and get back to work so he can finish it in time."

Dewey Dell rises, heaving to her feet. She looks down at the face. It is like a casting of fading bronze upon the pillow, the hands alone still with any semblance of life: a curled, gnarled inertness; a spent yet alert quality from which weariness, exhaustion, travail has not yet departed, as though they doubted even yet the actuality of rest, guarding with horned and penurious alertness the cessation which they know cannot last.

Dewey Dell stoops and slides the quilt from beneath them and draws it up over them to the chin, smoothing it down, drawing it smooth. Then without looking at pa she goes around the bed and leaves the room.

She will go out where Peabody is, where she can stand in the twilight and look at his back with such an expression that, feeling her eyes and turning, he will say: I would not let it grieve me, now. She was old, and sick too. Suffering more than we knew. She couldn't have got well. Vardaman's getting big now, and with you to take good care of them all. I would try not to let it grieve me. I expect you'd better go and get some supper ready. It dont have to be much. But they'll need to eat, and she looking at him, saying You could do so much for me if you just would. If you just knew. I am I and you are you and I know it and you dont know it and you could do so much for me if you just would and if you just would then I could tell you and then nobody would have to know it except you and me and Darl

Pa stands over the bed, dangle-armed, humped, motionless. He raises his hand to his head, scouring his hair, listening to the saw. He comes nearer and rubs his hand, palm and back, on his thigh and lays it on her face and then on the hump of quilt where her hands are. He touches the quilt as he saw Dewey Dell do, trying to smoothe it up to the chin, but disarranging it instead. He tries to smoothe it again, clumsily, his hand awkward as a claw, smoothing at the wrinkles which he made and which continue to emerge beneath his hand with perverse ubiquity, so that at last he desists, his hand falling to his side and stroking itself again, palm and back, on his thigh. The sound of the saw snores steadily into the room. Pa breathes with a quiet, rasping sound, mouthing the snuff against his gums. "God's will be done," he says. "Now I can get them teeth."

Jewel's hat droops limp about his neck, channelling water onto the soaked towsack tied about his shoulders as, ankle-deep in the running ditch, he pries with a slipping two-by-four, with a piece of rotting log for fulcrum, at the axle. Jewel, I say, she is dead, Jewel. Addie Bundren is dead

Vardaman

Then I begin to run. I run toward the back and come to the edge of the porch and stop. Then I begin to cry. I can feel where the fish was in the dust. It is cut up into pieces of not-fish now, not-blood on my hands and overalls. Then it wasn't so. It hadn't happened then. And now she is getting so far ahead I cannot catch her.

The trees look like chickens when they ruffle out into the cool dust on the hot days. If I jump off the porch I will be where the fish was, and it all cut up into not-fish now. I can hear the bed and her face and them and I can feel the floor shake when he walks on it that came and did it. That came and did it when she was all right but he came and did it.

"The fat son of a bitch."

I jump from the porch, running. The top of the barn comes swooping up out of the twilight. If I jump I can go through it like the pink lady in the circus, into the warm smelling, without having to wait. My hands grab at the bushes; beneath my feet the rocks and dirt go rubbling down.

Then I can breathe again, in the warm smelling. I enter the stall, trying to touch him, and then I can cry then I vomit the crying. As soon as he gets through kicking I can and then I can cry, the crying can.

"He kilt her. He kilt her."

The life in him runs under the skin, under my hand, running through the splotches, smelling up into my nose where the sickness is beginning to cry, vomiting the crying, and then I can breathe, vomiting it. It makes a lot of noise. I can smell the life running up from under my hands, up my arms, and then I can leave the stall.

I cannot find it. In the dark, along the dust, the walls I cannot find it. The crying makes a lot of noise. I wish it wouldn't make so much noise. Then I find it in the wagon shed, in the dust, and I run across the lot and into the road, the stick jouncing on my shoulder.

They watch me as I run up, beginning to jerk back, their eyes rolling, snorting, jerking back on the hitch-rein. I strike. I can hear the stick striking; I can see it hitting their heads, the breast-yoke, missing altogether sometimes as they rear and plunge, but I am glad.

"You kilt my maw!"

The stick breaks, they rearing and snorting, their feet popping loud on the ground; loud because it is going to rain and the air is empty for the rain. But it is still long enough. I run this way and that as they rear and jerk at the hitch-rein, striking.

"You kilt her!"

I strike at them, striking, they wheeling in a long lunge, the buggy wheeling onto two wheels and motionless like it is nailed to the ground and the horses motionless like they are nailed by the hind feet to the center of a whirling plate.

I run in the dust. I cannot see, running in the sucking dust where the buggy vanishes tilted on two wheels. I strike, the stick hitting into the ground, bouncing, striking into the dust and then into the air again and the dust sucking on down the road faster than if a car was in it. And then I can cry, looking at the stick. It is broken down to my hand, not longer than stove wood that was a long stick. I throw it away and I can cry. It does not make so much noise now.

The cow is standing in the barn door, chewing. When she sees me come into the lot she lows, her mouth full of flopping green, her tongue flopping.

"I aint a-goin to milk you. I aint a-goin to do nothing for them."

I hear her turn when I pass. When I turn she is just behind me with her sweet, hot, hard breath.

"Didn't I tell you I wouldn't?"

She nudges me, snuffing. She moans deep inside, her mouth closed. I jerk my hand, cursing her like Jewel does.

"Git, now."

I stoop my hand to the ground and run at her. She jumps back and whirls away and stops, watching me. She moans. She goes on to the path and stands there, looking up the path.

It is dark in the barn, warm, smelling, silent. I can
cry quietly, watching the top of the hill.

Cash comes to the hill, limping where he fell off
of the church. He looks down at the spring, then up
the road and back toward the barn. He comes down
the path stiffly and looks at the broken hitch-rein and
at the dust in the road and then up the road, where
the dust is gone.

"I hope they've got clean past Tull's by now. I so
hope hit."

Cash turns and limps up the path.

"Durn him. I showed him. Durn him."

I am not crying now. I am not anything. Dewey
Dell comes to the hill and calls me. Vardaman. I am
not anything. I am quiet. You, Vardaman. I can cry
quiet now, feeling and hearing my tears.

"Then hit want. Hit hadn't happened then. Hit was
a-layin right there on the ground. And now she's gittin ready to cook hit."

It is dark. I can hear wood, silence: I know them.
But not living sounds, not even him. It is as though
the dark were resolving him out of his integrity, into
an unrelated scattering of components—snuffings and
stampings; smells of cooling flesh and ammoniac hair;
an illusion of a co-ordinated whole of splotched hide
and strong bones within which, detached and secret
and familiar, an *is* different from my *is*. I see him dissolve—legs, a rolling eye, a gaudy splotching like cold
flames—and float upon the dark in fading solution;
all one yet neither; all either yet none. I can see hearing coil toward him, caressing, shaping his hard
shape—fetlock, hip, shoulder and head; smell and
sound. I am not afraid.

"Cooked and et. Cooked and et."

Dewey Dell

He could do so much for me if he just would. He could do everything for me. It's like everything in the world for me is inside a tub full of guts, so that you wonder how there can be any room in it for anything else very important. He is a big tub of guts and I am a little tub of guts and if there is not any room for anything else important in a big tub of guts, how can it be room in a little tub of guts. But I know it is there because God gave women a sign when something has happened bad.

It's because I am alone. If I could just feel it, it would be different, because I would not be alone. But if I were not alone, everybody would know it. And he could do so much for me, and then I would not be alone. Then I could be all right alone.

I would let him come in between me and Lafe, like Darl came in between me and Lafe, and so Lafe is alone too. He is Lafe and I am Dewey Dell, and when mother died I had to go beyond and outside of me and Lafe and Darl to grieve because he could do so much for me and he dont know it. He dont even know it.

From the back porch I cannot see the barn. Then the sound of Cash's sawing comes in from that way. It is like a dog outside the house, going back and forth around the house to whatever door you come to, waiting to come in. He said I worry more than you do and I said You dont know what worry is so I cant worry. I try to but I cant think long enough to worry.

I light the kitchen lamp. The fish, cut into jagged pieces, bleeds quietly in the pan. I put it into the cupboard quick, listening into the hall, hearing. It took her ten days to die; maybe she dont know it is yet. Maybe she wont go until Cash. Or maybe until Jewel. I take the dish of greens from the cupboard and the bread pan from the cold stove, and I stop, watching the door.

"Where's Vardaman?" Cash says. In the lamp his sawdusted arms look like sand.

"I dont know. I aint seen him."

"Peabody's team run away. See if you can find Vardaman. The horse will let him catch him."

"Well. Tell them to come to supper."

I cannot see the barn. I said, I dont know how to worry. I dont know how to cry. I tried, but I cant. After a while the sound of the saw comes around,

coming dark along the ground in the dust-dark. Then
I can see him, going up and down above the plank.

"You come in to supper," I say. "Tell him." He
could do everything for me. And he dont know it. He
is his guts and I am my guts. And I am Lafe's guts.
That's it. I dont see why he didn't stay in town. We
are country people, not as good as town people. I
dont see why he didn't. Then I can see the top of the
barn. The cow stands at the foot of the path, lowing.
When I turn back, Cash is gone.   Peabody

I carry the buttermilk in. Pa and Cash and (he) are
at the table.

"Where's that big fish Bud caught, sister?" he says.

I set the milk on the table. "I never had no time to
cook it."

"Plain turnip greens is mighty spindling eating for
a man my size," he says. Cash is eating. About his
head the print of his hat is sweated into his hair. His
shirt is blotched with sweat. He has not washed his
hands and arms.

"You ought to took time," pa says. "Where's Vardaman?"

I go toward the door. "I cant find him."

"Here, sister," he says; "never mind about the fish.
It'll save, I reckon. Come on and sit down."

"I aint minding it," I say. "I'm going to milk before
it sets in to rain."

Pa helps himself and pushes the dish on. But he
does not begin to eat. His hands are halfclosed on
either side of his plate, his head bowed a little, his
awry hair standing into the lamplight. He looks like
right after the maul hits the steer and it no longer
alive and dont yet know that it is dead.

But Cash is eating, and he is too. "You better eat

something," he says. He is looking at pa. "Like Cash and me. You'll need it."

"Ay," pa says. He rouses up, like a steer that's been kneeling in a pond and you run at it. "She would not begrudge me it."

When I am out of sight of the house, I go fast. The cow lows at the foot of the bluff. She nuzzles at me, snuffing, blowing her breath in a sweet, hot blast, through my dress, against my hot nakedness, moaning. "You got to wait a little while. Then I'll tend to you." She follows me into the barn where I set the bucket down. She breathes into the bucket, moaning. "I told you. You just got to wait, now. I got more to do than I can tend to." The barn is dark. When I pass, he kicks the wall a single blow. I go on. The broken plank is like a pale plank standing on end. Then I can see the slope, feel the air moving on my face again, slow, pale with lesser dark and with empty seeing, the pine clumps blotched up the tilted slope, secret and waiting.

The cow in silhouette against the door nuzzles at the silhouette of the bucket, moaning.

Then I pass the stall. I have almost passed it. I listen to it saying for a long time before it can say the word and the listening part is afraid that there may not be time to say it. I feel my body, my bones and flesh beginning to part and open upon the alone, and the process of coming unalone is terrible. Lafe. Lafe. "Lafe" Lafe. Lafe. I lean a little forward, one foot advanced with dead walking. I feel the darkness rushing past my breast, past the cow; I begin to rush upon the darkness but the cow stops me and the darkness rushes on upon the sweet blast of her moaning breath, filled with wood and with silence.

"Vardaman. You, Vardaman."

He comes out of the stall. "You durn little sneak! You durn little sneak!"

He does not resist; the last of rushing darkness flees whistling away. "What? I aint done nothing."

"You durn little sneak!" My hands shake him, hard. Maybe I couldn't stop them. I didn't know they could shake so hard. They shake both of us, shaking.

"I never done it," he says. "I never touched them."

My hands stop shaking him, but I still hold him. "What are you doing here? Why didn't you answer when I called you?"

"I aint doing nothing."

"You go on to the house and get your supper."

He draws back. I hold him. "You quit now. You leave me be."

"What were you doing down here? You didn't come down here to sneak after me?"

"I never. I never. You quit, now. I didn't even know you was down here. You leave me be."

I hold him, leaning down to see his face, feel it with my eyes. He is about to cry. "Go on, now. I done put supper on and I'll be there soon as I milk. You better go on before he eats everything up. I hope that team runs clean back to Jefferson."

"He kilt her," he says. He begins to cry.

"Hush."

"She never hurt him and he come and kilt her."

"Hush." He struggles. I hold him. "Hush."

"He kilt her." The cow comes up behind us, moaning. I shake him again.

"You stop it, now. Right this minute. You're fixing to make yourself sick and then you cant go to town. You go on to the house and eat your supper."

"I dont want no supper. I dont want to go to town."

"We'll leave you here, then. Lessen you behave, we
will leave you. Go on, now, before that old green-
eating tub of guts eats everything up from you." He
goes on, disappearing slowly into the hill. The crest,
the trees, the roof of the house stand against the sky.
The cow nuzzles at me, moaning. "You'll just have to
wait. What you got in you aint nothing to what I got
in me, even if you are a woman too." She follows me,
moaning. Then the dead, hot, pale air breathes on my
face again. He could fix it all right, if he just would.
And he dont even know it. He could do everything
for me if he just knowed it. The cow breathes upon
my hips and back, her breath warm, sweet, stertorous,
moaning. The sky lies flat down the slope, upon the
secret clumps. Beyond the hill sheet-lightning stains
upward and fades. The dead air shapes the dead earth
in the dead darkness, further away than seeing shapes
the dead earth. It lies dead and warm upon me, touching me naked through my clothes. I said You dont
know what worry is. I dont know what it is. I dont
know whether I am worrying or not. Whether I can
or not. I dont know whether I can cry or not. I dont
know whether I have tried to or not. I feel like a
wet seed wild in the hot blind earth.

Vardaman

When they get it finished they are going to put her in it and then for a long time I couldn't say it. I saw the dark stand up and go whirling away and I said "Are you going to nail her up in it, Cash? Cash? Cash?" I got shut up in the crib the new door it was too heavy for me it went shut I couldn't breathe because the rat was breathing up all the air. I said "Are you going to nail it shut, Cash? Nail it? *Nail* it?"

Pa walks around. His shadow walks around, over Cash going up and down above the saw, at the bleeding plank.

Dewey Dell said we will get some bananas. The train is behind the glass, red on the track. When it runs the track shines on and off. Pa said flour and sugar and coffee costs so much. Because I am a country boy because boys in town. Bicycles. Why do flour and sugar and coffee cost so much when he is a country boy. "Wouldn't you ruther have some bananas instead?" Bananas are gone, eaten. Gone. When it runs on the track shines again. "Why aint I a town boy, pa?" I said. God made me. I did not said to God to made me in the country. If He can make the train, why cant He make them all in the town because flour and sugar and coffee. "Wouldn't you ruther have bananas?"

He walks around. His shadow walks around.

It was not her. I was there, looking. I saw. I thought it was her, but it was not. It was not my mother. She went away when the other one laid down in her bed and drew the quilt up. She went away. "Did she go as far as town?" "She went further than town." "Did all those rabbits and possums go further than town?" God made the rabbits and possums. He made the train. Why must He make a different place for them to go if she is just like the rabbit.

Pa walks around. His shadow does. The saw sounds like it is asleep.

And so if Cash nails the box up, she is not a rabbit. And so if she is not a rabbit I couldn't breathe in the crib and Cash is going to nail it up. And so if she lets him it is not her. I know. I was there. I saw when it did not be her. I saw. They think it is and Cash is going to nail it up.

It was not her because it was laying right yonder in the dirt. And now it's all chopped up. I chopped it up. It's laying in the kitchen in the bleeding pan, waiting to be cooked and et. Then it wasn't and she was, and now it is and she wasn't. And tomorrow it will be cooked and et and she will be him and pa and Cash and Dewey Dell and there wont be anything in the box and so she can breathe. It was laying right yonder on the ground. I can get Vernon. He was there and he seen it, and with both of us it will be and then it will not be.

Tull

It was nigh to midnight and it had set into rain when he woke us. It had been a misdoubtful night, with the storm making; a night when a fellow looks for most anything to happen before he can get the stock fed and himself to the house and supper et and in bed with the rain starting, and when Peabody's team come up, lathered, with the broke harness dragging and the neck-yoke betwixt the off critter's legs, Cora says "It's Addie Bundren. She's gone at last."

"Peabody mought have been to ere a one of a dozen houses hereabouts," I says. "Besides, how do you know it's Peabody's team?"

"Well, aint it?" she says. "You hitch up, now."

"What for?" I says. "If she is gone, we cant do nothing till morning. And it fixing to storm, too."

"It's my duty," she says. "You put the team in."

But I wouldn't do it. "It stands to reason they'd send for us if they needed us. You dont even know she's gone yet."

"Why, dont you know that's Peabody's team? Do you claim it aint? Well, then." But I wouldn't go. When folks wants a fellow, it's best to wait till they sends for him, I've found. "It's my Christian duty," Cora says. "Will you stand between me and my Christian duty?"

"You can stay there all day tomorrow, if you want," I says.

So when Cora waked me it had set in to rain. Even while I was going to the door with the lamp and it shining on the glass so he could see I am coming, it kept on knocking. Not loud, but steady, like he might have gone to sleep thumping, but I never noticed how low down on the door the knocking was till I opened it and never seen nothing. I held the lamp up, with the rain sparkling across it and Cora back in the hall saying "Who is it, Vernon?" but I couldn't see nobody a-tall at first until I looked down and around the door, lowering the lamp.

He looked like a drownded puppy, in them overalls, without no hat, splashed up to his knees where he had walked them four miles in the mud. "Well, I'll be durned," I says.

"Who is it, Vernon?" Cora says.

He looked at me, his eyes round and black in the middle like when you throw a light in a owl's face. "You mind that ere fish," he says.

"Come in the house," I says. "What is it? Is your maw—"

"Vernon," Cora says.

He stood kind of around behind the door, in the dark. The rain was blowing onto the lamp, hissing on it so I am scared every minute it'll break. "You was there," he says. "You seen it."

Then Cora come to the door. "You come right in outen the rain," she says, pulling him in and him watching me. He looked just like a drownded puppy. "I told you," Cora says. "I told you it was a-happening. You go and hitch."

"But he aint said—" I says.

He looked at me, dripping onto the floor. "He's a-ruining the rug," Cora says. "You go get the team while I take him to the kitchen."

But he hung back, dripping, watching me with them eyes. "You was there. You seen it laying there. Cash is fixing to nail her up, and it was a-laying right there on the ground. You seen it. You seen the mark in the dirt. The rain never come up till after I was a-coming here. So we can get back in time."

I be durn if it didn't give me the creeps, even when I didn't know yet. But Cora did. "You get that team quick as you can," she says. "He's outen his head with grief and worry."

I be durn if it didn't give me the creeps. Now and then a fellow gets to thinking. About all the sorrow and afflictions in this world; how it's liable to strike anywhere, like lightning. I reckon it does take a powerful trust in the Lord to guard a fellow, though sometimes I think that Cora's a mite over-cautious, like she was trying to crowd the other folks away and get in closer than anybody else. But then, when something

like this happens, I reckon she is right and you got to
keep after it and I reckon I am blessed in having a
wife that ever strives for sanctity and well-doing like
she says I am.

Now and then a fellow gets to thinking about it.
Not often, though. Which is a good thing. For the
Lord aimed for him to do and not to spend too much
time thinking, because his brain it's like a piece of
machinery: it wont stand a whole lot of racking. It's
best when it all runs along the same, doing the day's
work and not no one part used no more than needful.
I have said and I say again, that's ever living thing
the matter with Darl: he just thinks by himself too
much. Cora's right when she says all he needs is a
wife to straighten him out. And when I think about
that, I think that if nothing but being married will
help a man, he's durn nigh hopeless. But I reckon
Cora's right when she says the reason the Lord had
to create women is because man dont know his own
good when he sees it.

When I come back to the house with the team, they
was in the kitchen. She was dressed on top of her
nightgownd, with a shawl over her head and her umbrella and her bible wrapped up in the oilcloth, and
him sitting on a up-turned bucket on the stove-zinc
where she had put him, dripping onto the floor. "I
cant get nothing outen him except about a fish," she
says. "It's a judgment on them. I see the hand of the
Lord upon this boy for Anse Bundren's judgment and
warning."

"The rain never come up till after I left," he says.
"I had done left. I was on the way. And so it was there
in the dust. You seen it. Cash is fixing to nail her, but
you seen it."

When we got there it was raining hard, and him sitting on the seat between us, wrapped up in Cora's shawl. He hadn't said nothing else, just sitting there with Cora holding the umbrella over him. Now and then Cora would stop singing long enough to say "It's a judgment on Anse Bundren. May it show him the path of sin he is a-trodding." Then she would sing again, and him sitting there between us, leaning forward a little like the mules couldn't go fast enough to suit him.

"It was laying right yonder," he says, "but the rain come up after I taken and left. So I can go and open the windows, because Cash aint nailed her yet."

It was long a-past midnight when we drove the last nail, and almost dust-dawn when I got back home and taken the team out and got back in bed, with Cora's nightcap laying on the other pillow. And be durned if even then it wasn't like I could still hear Cora singing and feel that boy leaning forward between us like he was ahead of the mules, and still see Cash going up and down with that saw, and Anse standing there like a scarecrow, like he was a steer standing knee-deep in a pond and somebody come by and set the pond up on edge and he aint missed it yet.

It was nigh toward daybreak when we drove the last nail and toted it into the house, where she was laying on the bed with the window open and the rain blowing on her again. Twice he did it, and him so dead for sleep that Cora says his face looked like one of these here Christmas masts that had done been buried a while and then dug up, until at last they put her into it and nailed it down so he couldn't open the window on her no more. And the next morning they found him in his shirt tail, laying asleep on the floor like a felled steer, and the top of the box bored clean full of holes and Cash's new auger broke off in the last one. When they taken the lid off they found that two of them had bored on into her face.

If it's a judgment, it aint right. Because the Lord's got more to do than that. He's bound to have. Because the only burden Anse Bundren's ever had is himself. And when folks talks him low, I think to myself he aint that less of a man or he couldn't a bore himself this long.

It aint right. I be durn if it is. Because He said Suffer little children to come unto Me dont make it right, neither. Cora said, "I have bore you what the Lord God sent me. I faced it without fear nor terror because my faith was strong in the Lord, a-bolstering and sustaining me. If you have no son, it's because the Lord has decreed otherwise in His wisdom. And my life is and has ever been a open book to ere a man or woman among His creatures because I trust in my God and my reward."

I reckon she's right. I reckon if there's ere a man or woman anywhere that He could turn it all over to and go away with His mind at rest, it would be Cora. And I reckon she would make a few changes, no matter how He was running it. And I reckon they would be for man's good. Leastways, we would have to like them. Leastways, we might as well go on and make like we did.

Darl

The lantern sits on a stump. Rusted, grease-fouled, its cracked chimney smeared on one side with a soaring smudge of soot, it sheds a feeble and sultry glare upon the trestles and the boards and the adjacent earth. Upon the dark ground the chips look like random smears of soft pale paint on a black canvas. The boards look like long smooth tatters torn from the flat darkness and turned backside out.

Cash labors about the trestles, moving back and forth, lifting and placing the planks with long clattering reverberations in the dead air as though he were lifting and dropping them at the bottom of an invisible well, the sounds ceasing without departing, as if any movement might dislodge them from the immediate air in reverberant repetition. He saws again, his elbow flashing slowly, a thin thread of fire running along the edge of the saw, lost and recovered at the top and bottom of each stroke in unbroken elongation, so that the saw appears to be six feet long, into and out of pa's shabby and aimless silhouette. "Give me that plank," Cash says. "No; the other one." He puts the saw down and comes and picks up the plank he wants, sweeping pa away with the long swinging gleam of the balanced board.

The air smells like sulphur. Upon the impalpable plane of it their shadows form as upon a wall, as though like sound they had not gone very far away in falling but had merely congealed for a moment, immediate and musing. Cash works on, half turned into the feeble light, one thigh and one pole-thin arm braced, his face sloped into the light with a rapt, dynamic immobility above his tireless elbow. Below the sky sheet-lightning slumbers lightly; against it the trees, motionless, are ruffled out to the last twig, swollen, increased as though quick with young.

It begins to rain. The first harsh, sparse, swift drops rush through the leaves and across the ground in a long sigh, as though of relief from intolerable suspense. They are big as buckshot, warm as though fired from a gun; they sweep across the lantern in a vicious hissing. Pa lifts his face, slack-mouthed, the wet black rim of snuff plastered close along the base of his gums; from behind his slack-faced astonishment he muses as though from beyond time, upon the ultimate outrage. Cash looks once at the sky, then at the lantern. The saw has not faltered, the running gleam of its pistoning edge unbroken. "Get something to cover the lantern," he says.

Pa goes to the house. The rain rushes suddenly down, without thunder, without warning of any sort; he is swept onto the porch upon the edge of it and in an instant Cash is wet to the skin. Yet the motion of the saw has not faltered, as though it and the arm functioned in a tranquil conviction that rain was an illusion of the mind. Then he puts down the saw and goes and crouches above the lantern, shielding it with his body, his back shaped lean and scrawny by his wet shirt as though he had been abruptly turned wrong-side out, shirt and all.

Pa returns. He is wearing Jewel's raincoat and carrying Dewey Dell's. Squatting over the lantern, Cash reaches back and picks up four sticks and drives them into the earth and takes Dewey Dell's raincoat from pa and spreads it over the sticks, forming a roof above the lantern. Pa watches him. "I dont know what you'll do," he says. "Darl taken his coat with him."

"Get wet," Cash says. He takes up the saw again; again it moves up and down, in and out of that un-hurried imperviousness as a piston moves in the oil; soaked, scrawny, tireless, with the lean light body of a boy or an old man. Pa watches him, blinking, his face streaming; again he looks up at the sky with that expression of dumb and brooding outrage and yet of vindication, as though he had expected no less; now and then he stirs, moves, gaunt and streaming, pick-ing up a board or a tool and then laying it down. Ver-non Tull is there now, and Cash is wearing Mrs Tull's raincoat and he and Vernon are hunting the saw. After a while they find it in pa's hand.

"Why dont you go on to the house, out of the rain?" Cash says. Pa looks at him, his face streaming slowly. It is as though upon a face carved by a savage cari-

caturist a monstrous burlesque of all bereavement
flowed. "You go on in," Cash says. "Me and Vernon
can finish it."

Pa looks at them. The sleeves of Jewel's coat are
too short for him. Upon his face the rain streams, slow
as cold glycerin. "I dont begrudge her the wetting," he
says. He moves again and falls to shifting the planks,
picking them up, laying them down again carefully,
as though they are glass. He goes to the lantern and
pulls at the propped raincoat until he knocks it down
and Cash comes and fixes it back.

"You get on to the house," Cash says. He leads pa
to the house and returns with the raincoat and folds
it and places it beneath the shelter where the lantern
sits. Vernon has not stopped. He looks up, still sawing.

"You ought to done that at first," he says. "You
knowed it was fixing to rain."

"It's his fever," Cash says. He looks at the board.

"Ay," Vernon says. "He'd a come, anyway."

Cash squints at the board. On the long flank of it
the rain crashes steadily, myriad, fluctuant. "I'm going
to bevel it," he says.

"It'll take more time," Vernon says. Cash sets the
plank on edge; a moment longer Vernon watches him,
then he hands him the plane.

Vernon holds the board steady while Cash bevels
the edge of it with the tedious and minute care of a
jeweler. Mrs Tull comes to the edge of the porch and
calls Vernon. "How near are you done?" she says.

Vernon does not look up. "Not long. Some, yet."

She watches Cash stooping at the plank, the turgid
savage gleam of the lantern slicking on the raincoat
as he moves. "You go down and get some planks off
the barn and finish it and come in out of the rain," she

says. "You'll both catch your death." Vernon does not move. "Vernon," she says.

"We wont be long," he says. "We'll be done after a spell." Mrs Tull watches them a while. Then she re-enters the house.

"If we get in a tight, we could take some of them planks," Vernon says. "I'll help you put them back."

Cash ceases the plane and squints along the plank, wiping it with his palm. "Give me the next one," he says.

Some time toward dawn the rain ceases. But it is not yet day when Cash drives the last nail and stands stiffly up and looks down at the finished coffin, the others watching him. In the lantern light his face is calm, musing; slowly he strokes his hands on his rain-coated thighs in a gesture deliberate, final and com-posed. Then the four of them—Cash and pa and Ver-non and Peabody—raise the coffin to their shoulders and turn toward the house. It is light, yet they move slowly; empty, yet they carry it carefully; lifeless, yet they move with hushed precautionary words to one another, speaking of it as though, complete, it now slumbered lightly alive, waiting to come awake. On the dark floor their feet clump awkwardly, as though for a long time they have not walked on floors.

They set it down by the bed. Peabody says quietly: "Let's eat a snack. It's almost daylight. Where's Cash?"

He has returned to the trestles, stooped again in the lantern's feeble glare as he gathers up his tools and wipes them on a cloth carefully and puts them into the box with its leather sling to go over the shoulder. Then he takes up box, lantern and raincoat and re-turns to the house, mounting the steps into faint sil-houette against the paling east.

In a strange room you must empty yourself for sleep. And before you are emptied for sleep, what are you. And when you are emptied for sleep, you are not. And when you are filled with sleep, you never were. I dont know what I am. I dont know if I am or not. Jewel knows he *is*, because he does not know that he does not know whether he is or not. He cannot empty himself for sleep because he is not what he is and he is what he is not. Beyond the unlamped wall I can hear the rain shaping the wagon that is ours, the load that is no longer theirs that felled and sawed it nor yet theirs that bought it and which is not ours either, lie on our wagon though it does, since only the wind and the rain shape it only to Jewel and me, that are not asleep. And since sleep is is-not and rain and wind are *was*, it is not. Yet the wagon *is*, because when the wagon is *was*, Addie Bundren will not be. And Jewel *is*, so Addie Bundren must be. And then I must be, or I could not empty myself for sleep in a strange room. And so if I am not emptied yet, I am *is*.

How often have I lain beneath rain on a strange roof, thinking of home.

Cash

I made it on the bevel.
1. There is more surface for the nails to grip.
2. There is twice the gripping-surface to each seam.
3. The water will have to seep into it on a slant. Water moves easiest up and down or straight across.
4. In a house people are upright two thirds of the time. So the seams and joints are made up-and-down. Because the stress is up-and-down.
5. In a bed where people lie down all the time, the joints and seams are made sideways, because the stress is sideways.
6. Except.
7. A body is not square like a crosstie.

8. Animal magnetism.
9. The animal magnetism of a dead body makes the stress come slanting, so the seams and joints of a coffin are made on the bevel.
10. You can see by an old grave that the earth sinks down on the bevel.
11. While in a natural hole it sinks by the center, the stress being up-and-down.
12. So I made it on the bevel.
13. It makes a neater job.

13. - Doesn't care about unlucky 13. Doesn't matter to Cash

Vardaman

My mother is a fish.

Tull

20

It was ten oclock when I got back, with Peabody's team hitched on to the back of the wagon. They had already dragged the buckboard back from where Quick found it upside down straddle of the ditch about a mile from the spring. It was pulled out of the road at the spring, and about a dozen wagons was already there. It was Quick found it. He said the river was up and still rising. He said it had already covered the highest water-mark on the bridge-piling he had ever seen. "That bridge wont stand a whole lot of water," I said. "Has somebody told Anse about it?"

"I told him," Quick said. "He says he reckons them boys has heard and unloaded and are on the way back by now. He says they can load up and get across."

"He better go on and bury her at New Hope," Armstid said. "That bridge is old. I wouldn't monkey with it."

"His mind is set on taking her to Jefferson," Quick said.

"Then he better get at it soon as he can," Armstid said.

Anse meets us at the door. He has shaved, but not good. There is a long cut on his jaw, and he is wearing his Sunday pants and a white shirt with the neckband buttoned. It is drawn smooth over his hump, making it look bigger than ever, like a white shirt will, and his face is different too. He looks folks in the eye now, dignified, his face tragic and composed, shaking us by the hand as we walk up onto the porch and scrape our shoes, a little stiff in our Sunday clothes, our Sunday clothes rustling, not looking full at him as he meets us.

"The Lord giveth," we say.

"The Lord giveth."

That boy is not there. Peabody told about how he come into the kitchen, hollering, swarming and clawing at Cora when he found her cooking that fish, and how Dewey Dell taken him down to the barn. "My team all right?" Peabody says.

"All right," I tell him. "I give them a bait this morning. Your buggy seems all right too. It aint hurt."

"And no fault of somebody's," he says. "I'd give a nickel to know where that boy was when that team broke away."

"If it's broke anywhere, I'll fix it," I say.

The women folks go on into the house. We can hear them, talking and fanning. The fans go whish. whish. whish and them talking, the talking sounding kind of like bees murmuring in a water bucket. The men stop on the porch, talking some, not looking at one another.

"Howdy, Vernon," they say. "Howdy, Tull."

"Looks like more rain."

"It does for a fact."

"Yes, sir. It will rain some more."

"It come up quick."

"And going away slow. It dont fail."

I go around to the back. Cash is filling up the holes he bored in the top of it. He is trimming out plugs for them, one at a time, the wood wet and hard to work. He could cut up a tin can and hide the holes and nobody wouldn't know the difference. Wouldn't mind, anyway. I have seen him spend a hour trimming out a wedge like it was glass he was working, when he could have reached around and picked up a dozen sticks and drove them into the joint and made it do.

When we finished I go back to the front. The men have gone a little piece from the house, sitting on the ends of the boards and on the sawhorses where we made it last night, some sitting and some squatting. Whitfield aint come yet.

They look up at me, their eyes asking.

"It's about," I say. "He's ready to nail."

While they are getting up Anse comes to the door and looks at us and we return to the porch. We scrape our shoes again, careful, waiting for one another to go in first, milling a little at the door. Anse stands inside the door, dignified, composed. He waves us in and leads the way into the room.

They had laid her in it reversed. Cash made it clock-shape, like this ⬡ with every joint and seam bevelled and scrubbed with the plane, tight as a drum and neat as a sewing basket, and they had laid her in it head to foot so it wouldn't crush her dress. It was her wedding dress and it had a flare-out bottom, and they had laid her head to foot in it so the dress could spread out, and they had made her a veil out of a mosquito bar so the auger holes in her face wouldn't show.

When we are going out, Whitfield comes. He is wet and muddy to the waist, coming in. "The Lord comfort this house," he says. "I was late because the bridge has gone. I went down to the old ford and swum my horse over, the Lord protecting me. His grace be upon this house."

We go back to the trestles and plank-ends and sit or squat.

"I knowed it would go," Armstid says.

"It's been there a long time, that ere bridge," Quick says.

"The Lord has kept it there, you mean," Uncle Billy says. "I dont know ere a man that's touched hammer to it in twenty-five years."

"How long has it been there, Uncle Billy?" Quick says.

"It was built in . . . let me see . . . It was in the year 1888," Uncle Billy says. "I mind it because the first man to cross it was Peabody coming to my house when Jody was born."

"If I'd a crossed it every time your wife littered since, it'd a been wore out long before this, Billy," Peabody says.

We laugh, suddenly loud, then suddenly quiet again. We look a little aside at one another.

"Lots of folks has crossed it that wont cross no more bridges," Houston says.

"It's a fact," Littlejohn says. "It's so."

"One more aint, no ways," Armstid says. "It'd taken them two-three days to got her to town in the wagon. They'd be gone a week, getting her to Jefferson and back."

"What's Anse so itching to take her to Jefferson for, anyway?" Houston says.

"He promised her," I say. "She wanted it. She come from there. Her mind was set on it."

"And Anse is set on it, too," Quick says.

"Ay," Uncle Billy says. "It's like a man that's let everything slide all his life to get set on something that will make the most trouble for everybody he knows."

"Well, it'll take the Lord to get her over that river now," Peabody says. "Anse cant do it."

"And I reckon He will," Quick says. "He's took care of Anse a long time, now."

"It's a fact," Littlejohn says.

"Too long to quit now," Armstid says.

"I reckon He's like everybody else around here," Uncle Billy says. "He's done it so long now He cant quit."

Cash comes out. He has put on a clean shirt; his hair, wet, is combed smooth down on his brow, smooth and black as if he had painted it onto his head. He squats stiffly among us, we watching him.

"You feeling this weather, aint you?" Armstid says.

Cash says nothing.

"A broke bone always feels it," Littlejohn says. "A fellow with a broke bone can tell it a-coming."

"Lucky Cash got off with just a broke leg," Armstid says. "He might have hurt himself bed-rid. How far'd you fall, Cash?"

"Twenty-eight foot, four and a half inches Cash says. I move over beside him.

"A fellow can sho slip quick on wet planks," .uck says.

"It's too bad," I say. "But you couldn't a holp it."

"It's them durn women," he says. "I made it to balance with her. I made it to her measure and weight."

If it takes wet boards for folks to fall, it's fixing to be lots of falling before this spell is done.

"You couldn't have holp it," I say.

I dont mind the folks falling. It's the cotton and corn I mind.

Neither does Peabody mind the folks falling. How bout it, Doc?

It's a fact. Washed clean outen the ground it will be. Seems like something is always happening to it.

Course it does. That's why it's worth anything. If nothing didn't happen and everybody made a big crop, do you reckon it would be worth the raising?

Well, I be durn if I like to see my work washed outen the ground, work I sweat over.

It's a fact. A fellow wouldn't mind seeing it washed up if he could just turn on the rain himself.

Who is that man can do that? Where is the color of his eyes?

Ay. The Lord made it to grow. It's Hisn to wash up if He sees it fitten so.

"You couldn't have holp it," I say.

"It's them durn women," he says.

In the house the women begin to sing. We hear the first line commence, beginning to swell as they take hold, and we rise and move toward the door, taking off our hats and throwing our chews away. We do not go in. We stop at the steps, clumped, holding our hats

between our lax hands in front or behind, standing
with one foot advanced and our heads lowered, looking aside, down at our hats in our hands and at the
earth or now and then at the sky and at one another's
grave, composed face.

The song ends; the voices quaver away with a rich
and dying fall. Whitfield begins. His voice is bigger
than him. It's like they are not the same. It's like he
is one, and his voice is one, swimming on two horses
side by side across the ford and coming into the house,
the mud-splashed one and the one that never even got
wet, triumphant and sad. Somebody in the house begins to cry. It sounds like her eyes and her voice were
turned back inside her, listening; we move, shifting
to the other leg, meeting one another's eye and making like they hadn't touched.

Whitfield stops at last. The women sing again. In
the thick air it's like their voices come out of the air,
flowing together and on in the sad, comforting tunes.
When they cease it's like they hadn't gone away. It's
like they had just disappeared into the air and when
we moved we would loose them again out of the air
around us, sad and comforting. Then they finish and
we put on our hats, our movements stiff, like we hadn't
never wore hats before.

On the way home Cora is still singing. "I am bounding toward my God and my reward," she sings, sitting on the wagon, the shawl around her shoulders
and the umbrella open over her, though it is not raining.

"She has hern," I say. "Wherever she went, she has
her reward in being free of Anse Bundren." *She laid
there three days in that box, waiting for Darl and
Jewel to come clean back home and get a new wheel*

and go back to where the wagon was in the ditch. Take my team, Anse, I said.

We'll wait for ourn, he said. She'll want it so. She was ever a particular woman.

On the third day they got back and they loaded her into the wagon and started and it already too late. You'll have to go all the way round by Samson's bridge. It'll take you a day to get there. Then you'll be forty miles from Jefferson. Take my team, Anse.

We'll wait for ourn. She'll want it so.

It was about a mile from the house we saw him, sitting on the edge of the slough. It hadn't had a fish in it never that I knowed. He looked around at us, his eyes round and calm, his face dirty, the pole across his knees. Cora was still singing.

"This aint no good day to fish," I said. "You come on home with us and me and you'll go down to the river first thing in the morning and catch some fish."

"It's one in here," he said. "Dewey Dell seen it."

"You come on with us. The river's the best place."

"It's in here," he said. "Dewey Dell seen it."

"I'm bounding toward my God and my reward," Cora sung.

Darl

"It's not your horse that's dead, Jewel," I say. He sits erect on the seat, leaning a little forward, wooden-backed. The brim of his hat has soaked free of the crown in two places, drooping across his wooden face so that, head lowered, he looks through it like through the visor of a helmet, looking long across the valley to where the barn leans against the bluff, shaping the invisible horse. "See them?" I say. High above the house, against the quick thick sky, they hang in narrowing circles. From here they are no more than specks, implacable, patient, portentous. "But it's not your horse that's dead."

"Goddamn you," he says. "Goddamn you."

I cannot love my mother because I have no mother. Jewel's mother is a horse.

Motionless, the tall buzzards hang in soaring circles, the clouds giving them an illusion of retrograde.

Motionless, wooden-backed, wooden-faced, he shapes the horse in a rigid stoop like a hawk, hook-winged. They are waiting for us, ready for the moving of it, waiting for him. He enters the stall and waits until it kicks at him so that he can slip past and mount onto the trough and pause, peering out across the intervening stall-tops toward the empty path, before he reaches into the loft.

"Goddamn him. Goddamn him."

Cash

"It wont balance. If you want it to tote and ride on a balance, we will have—"

"Pick up. Goddamn you, pick up."

"I'm telling you it wont tote and it wont ride on a balance unless—"

"Pick up! Pick up, goddamn your thick-nosed soul to hell, pick up!"

It wont balance. If they want it to tote and ride on a balance, they will have

Darl

He stoops among us above it, two of the eight hands. In his face the blood goes in waves. In between them his flesh is greenish looking, about that smooth, thick, pale green of cow's cud; his face suffocated, furious, his lip lifted upon his teeth. "Pick up!" he says. "Pick up, goddamn your thick-nosed soul!"

He heaves, lifting one whole side so suddenly that we all spring into the lift to catch and balance it before he hurls it completely over. For an instant it resists, as though volitional, as though within it her pole-thin body clings furiously, even though dead, to a sort of modesty, as she would have tried to conceal a soiled garment that she could not prevent her body soiling. Then it breaks free, rising suddenly as though the

emaciation of her body had added buoyancy to the
planks or as though, seeing that the garment was about
to be torn from her, she rushes suddenly after it in a
passionate reversal that flouts its own desire and need.
Jewel's face goes completely green and I can hear
teeth in his breath.

We carry it down the hall, our feet harsh and
clumsy on the floor, moving with shuffling steps, and
through the door.

"Steady it a minute, now," pa says, letting go. He
turns back to shut and lock the door, but Jewel will
not wait.

"Come on," he says in that suffocating voice. "Come
on."

We lower it carefully down the steps. We move,
balancing it as though it were something infinitely precious, our faces averted, breathing through our teeth
to keep our nostrils closed. We go down the path, toward the slope.

"We better wait," Cash says. "I tell you it aint balanced now. We'll need another hand on that hill."

"Then turn loose," Jewel says. He will not stop. Cash
begins to fall behind, hobbling to keep up, breathing
harshly; then he is distanced and Jewel carries the
entire front end alone, so that, tilting as the path begins to slant, it begins to rush away from me and slip
down the air like a sled upon invisible snow, smoothly
evacuating atmosphere in which the sense of it is still
shaped.

"Wait, Jewel," I say. But he will not wait. He is
almost running now and Cash is left behind. It seems
to me that the end which I now carry alone has no
weight, as though it coasts like a rushing straw upon
the furious tide of Jewel's despair. I am not even

touching it when, turning, he lets it overshoot him, swinging, and stops it and sloughs it into the wagon bed in the same motion and looks back at me, his face suffused with fury and despair.

"Goddamn you. Goddamn you."

Vardaman

We are going to town. Dewey Dell says it wont be sold because it belongs to Santa Claus and he taken it back with him until next Christmas. Then it will be behind the glass again, shining with waiting.

Pa and Cash are coming down the hill, but Jewel is going to the barn. "Jewel," pa says. Jewel does not stop. "Where you going?" pa says. But Jewel does not stop. "You leave that horse here," pa says. Jewel stops and looks at pa. Jewel's eyes look like marbles. "You leave that horse here," pa says. "We'll all go in the wagon with ma, like she wanted."

But my mother is a fish. Vernon seen it. He was there.

"Jewel's mother is a horse," Darl said.

"Then mine can be a fish, cant it, Darl?" I said.

Jewel is my brother.

"Then mine will have to be a horse, too," I said.

"Why?" Darl said. "If pa is your pa, why does your ma have to be a horse just because Jewel's is?"

"Why does it?" I said. "Why does it, Darl?"

Darl is my brother.

"Then what is your ma, Darl?" I said.

"I haven't got ere one," Darl said. "Because if I had one, it is *was*. And if it is was, it cant be *is*. Can it?"

"No," I said.

"Then I am not," Darl said. "Am I?"

"No," I said.

I am. Darl is my brother.

"But you *are*, Darl," I said.

"I know it," Darl said. "That's why I am not *is*. *Are* is too many for one woman to foal."

Cash is carrying his tool box. Pa looks at him. "I'll stop at Tull's on the way back," Cash says. "Get on that barn roof."

"It aint respectful," pa says. "It's a deliberate flouting of her and of me."

"Do you want him to come all the way back here and carry them up to Tull's afoot?" Darl says. Pa looks at Darl, his mouth chewing. Pa shaves every day now because my mother is a fish.

"It aint right," pa says.

Dewey Dell has the package in her hand. She has the basket with our dinner too.

"What's that?" pa says.

"Mrs Tull's cakes," Dewey Dell says, getting into the wagon. "I'm taking them to town for her."

"It aint right," pa says. "It's a flouting of the dead."

It'll be there. It'll be there come Christmas, she says, shining on the track. She says he wont sell it to no town boys.

Darl

25

He goes on toward the barn, entering the lot, wooden-backed.

Dewey Dell carries the basket on one arm, in the other hand something wrapped square in a newspaper. Her face is calm and sullen, her eyes brooding and alert; within them I can see Peabody's back like two round peas in two thimbles: perhaps in Peabody's back two of those worms which work surreptitious and steady through you and out the other side and you waking suddenly from sleep or from waking, with on your face an expression sudden, intent, and concerned. She sets the basket into the wagon and climbs in, her leg coming long from beneath her tightening dress: that lever which moves the world; one of that caliper which measures the length and breadth of life. She sits on the seat beside Vardaman and sets the parcel on her lap.

Then he enters the barn. He has not looked back.

"It aint right," pa says. "It's little enough for him to do for her."

"Go on," Cash says. "Leave him stay if he wants. He'll be all right here. Maybe he'll go up to Tull's and stay."

"He'll catch us," I say. "He'll cut across and meet us at Tull's lane."

"He would have rid that horse, too," pa says, "if I hadn't a stopped him. A durn spotted critter wilder than a cattymount. A deliberate flouting of her and of me."

The wagon moves; the mules' ears begin to bob. Behind us, above the house, motionless in tall and soaring circles, they diminish and disappear.

Anse

I told him not to bring that horse out of respect for his dead ma, because it wouldn't look right, him prancing along on a durn circus animal and her wanting us all to be in the wagon with her that sprung from her flesh and blood, but we hadn't no more than passed Tull's lane when Darl begun to laugh. Setting back there on the plank seat with Cash, with his dead ma laying in her coffin at his feet, laughing. How many times I told him it's doing such things as that that makes folks talk about him. I dont know. I says I got some regard for what folks says about my flesh and blood even if you haven't, even if I have raised such a durn passel of boys, and when you fixes it so folks can say such about you, it's a reflection on your

ma, I says, not me: I am a man and I can stand it; it's
on your womenfolks, your ma and sister that you
should care for, and I turned and looked back at him
and him setting there, laughing.

"I dont expect you to have no respect for me," I says.
"But with your own ma not cold in her coffin yet."

"Yonder," Cash says, jerking his head toward the
lane. The horse is still a right smart piece away, coming up at a good pace, but I dont have to be told who
it is. I just looked back at Darl, setting there laughing.

"I done my best," I says. "I tried to do as she would
wish it. The Lord will pardon me and excuse the conduct of them He sent me." And Darl setting on the
plank seat right above her where she was laying,
laughing.

Darl

He comes up the lane fast, yet we are three hundred yards beyond the mouth of it when he turns into the road, the mud flying beneath the flicking drive of the hooves. Then he slows a little, light and erect in the saddle, the horse mincing through the mud.

Tull is in his lot. He looks at us, lifts his hand. We go on, the wagon creaking, the mud whispering on the wheels. Vernon still stands there. He watches Jewel as he passes, the horse moving with a light, high-kneed driving gait, three hundred yards back. We go on, with a motion so soporific, so dreamlike as to be uninferant of progress, as though time and not space were decreasing between us and it.

It turns off at right angles, the wheel-marks of last Sunday healed away now: a smooth, red scoriation curving away into the pines; a white signboard with faded lettering: New Hope Church. 3 mi. It wheels up like a motionless hand lifted above the profound desolation of the ocean; beyond it the red road lies like a spoke of which Addie Bundren is the rim. It wheels past, empty, unscarred, the white signboard turns away its fading and tranquil assertion. Cash looks up the road quietly, his head turning as we pass it like an owl's head, his face composed. Pa looks straight ahead, humped. Dewey Dell looks at the road too, then she looks back at me, her eyes watchful and repudiant, not like that question which was in those of Cash, for a smoldering while. The signboard passes; the unscarred road wheels on. Then Dewey Dell turns her head. The wagon creaks on.

Cash spits over the wheel. "In a couple of days now it'll be smelling," he says.

"You might tell Jewel that," I say.

He is motionless now, sitting the horse at the junction, upright, watching us, no less still than the signboard that lifts its fading capitulation opposite him.

"It aint balanced right for no long ride," Cash says.

"Tell him that, too," I say. The wagon creaks on.

A mile further along he passes us, the horse, arch-necked, reined back to a swift singlefoot. He sits lightly, poised, upright, wooden-faced in the saddle, the broken hat raked at a swaggering angle. He passes us swiftly, without looking at us, the horse driving, its hooves hissing in the mud. A gout of mud, back-flung, plops onto the box. Cash leans forward and takes a tool from his box and removes it carefully.

When the road crosses Whiteleaf, the willows leaning near enough, he <u>breaks off a branch and scours</u> at
<u>the stain with the wet leaves.</u>

Anse 28

It's a hard country on man; it's hard. Eight miles of the sweat of his body washed up outen the Lord's earth, where the Lord Himself told him to put it. Nowhere in this sinful world can a honest, hardworking man profit. It takes them that runs the stores in the towns, doing no sweating, living off of them that sweats. It aint the hardworking man, the farmer. Sometimes I wonder why we keep at it. It's because there is a reward for us above, where they cant take their autos and such. Every man will be equal there and it will be taken from them that have and give to them that have not by the Lord.

But it's a long wait, seems like. It's bad that a fellow must earn the reward of his right-doing by

flouting hisself and his dead. We drove all the rest of
the day and <u>got to Samson's at dust-dark</u> and then
<u>that bridge was gone, too.</u> They hadn't never see the
river so high, and it not done raining yet. There was
old men that hadn't never see nor hear of it being
so in the memory of man. I am the chosen of the
Lord, for who He loveth, so doeth He chastiseth. But
I be durn if He dont take some curious ways to show
it, seems like.

But now I can get them teeth. That will be a comfort. It will.

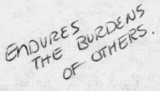

Samson

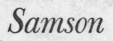

It was just before sundown. We were sitting on the porch when the wagon came up the road with the five of them in it and the other one on the horse behind. One of them raised his hand, but they was going on past the store without stopping.

"Who's that?" MacCallum says: I cant think of his name: Rafe's twin; that one it was.

"It's Bundren, from down beyond New Hope," Quick says. "There's one of them Snopes horses Jewel's riding."

"I didn't know there was ere a one of them horses left," MacCallum says. "I thought you folks down there finally contrived to give them all away."

"Try and get that one," Quick says. The wagon went on.

"I bet old man Lon never gave it to him," I says.

"No," Quick says. "He bought it from pappy." The wagon went on. "They must not a heard about the bridge," he says.

"What're they doing up here, anyway?" MacCallum says.

"Taking a holiday since he got his wife buried, I reckon," Quick says. "Heading for town, I reckon, with Tull's bridge gone too. I wonder if they aint heard about the bridge."

"They'll have to fly, then," I says. "I dont reckon there's ere a bridge between here and Mouth of Ishatawa."

They had something in the wagon. But Quick had been to the funeral three days ago and we naturally never thought anything about it except that they were heading away from home mighty late and that they hadn't heard about the bridge. "You better holler at them," MacCallum says. Durn it, the name is right on the tip of my tongue. So Quick hollered and they stopped and he went to the wagon and told them.

He come back with them. "They're going to Jefferson," he says. "The bridge at Tull's is gone, too." Like we didn't know it, and his face looked funny, around the nostrils, but they just sat there, Bundren and the girl and the chap on the seat, and Cash and the second one, the one folks talks about, on a plank across the tail-gate, and the other one on that spotted horse. But I reckon they was used to it by then, because when I said to Cash that they'd have to pass by New Hope again and what they'd better do, he just says,

"I reckon we can get there."

I aint much for meddling. Let every man run his own business to suit himself, I say. But after I talked to Rachel about them not having a regular man to fix her and it being July and all, I went back down to the barn and tried to talk to Bundren about it.

"I give her my promise," he says. "Her mind was set on it."

I notice how it takes a lazy man, a man that hates moving, to get set on moving once he does get started off, the same as he was set on staying still, like it aint the moving he hates so much as the starting and the stopping. And like he would be kind of proud of whatever come up to make the moving or the setting still look hard. He set there on the wagon, hunched up, blinking, listening to us tell about how quick the bridge went and how high the water was, and I be durn if he didn't act like he was proud of it, like he had made the river rise himself.

"You say it's higher than you ever see it before?" he says. "God's will be done," he says. "I reckon it wont go down much by morning, neither," he says.

"You better stay here tonight," I says, "and get a early start for New Hope tomorrow morning." I was just sorry for them bone-gaunted mules. I told Rachel, I says, "Well, would you have had me turn them away at dark, eight miles from home? What else could I do," I says. "It wont be but one night, and they'll keep it in the barn, and they'll sholy get started by daylight." And so I says, "You stay here tonight and early tomorrow you can go back to New Hope. I got tools enough, and the boys can go on right after supper and have it dug and ready if they want" and then I found that girl watching me. If her eyes had a been

pistols, I wouldn't be talking now. I be dog if they
didn't blaze at me. And so when I went down to the
barn I come on them, her talking so she never noticed
when I come up.

"You promised her," she says. "She wouldn't go
until you promised. She thought she could depend on
you. If you dont do it, it will be a curse on you."

"Cant no man say I dont aim to keep my word,"
Bundren says. "My heart is open to ere a man."

"I dont care what your heart is," she says. She was
whispering, kind of, talking fast. "You promised her.
You've got to. You—" then she seen me and quit,
standing there. If they'd been pistols, I wouldn't be
talking now. So when I talked to him about it, he says,

"I give her my promise. Her mind is set on it."

"But seems to me she'd rather have her ma buried
close by, so she could—"   ✗

"It's Addie I give the promise to," he says. "Her
mind is set on it."

So I told them to drive it into the barn, because it
was threatening rain again, and that supper was about
ready. Only they didn't want to come in.

"I thank you," Bundren says. "We wouldn't dis-
commode you. We got a little something in the basket.
We can make out."

"Well," I says, "since you are so particular about
your womenfolks, I am too. And when folks stops
with us at meal time and wont come to the table, my
wife takes it as a insult."

So the girl went on to the kitchen to help Rachel.
And then Jewel come to me.

"Sho," I says. "Help yourself outen the loft. Feed
him when you bait the mules."

"I rather pay you for him," he says.

"What for?" I says. "I wouldn't begrudge no man a bait for his horse."

"I rather pay you," he says; I thought he said extra.

"Extra for what?" I says. "Wont he eat hay and corn?"

"Extra feed," he says. "I feed him a little extra and I dont want him beholden to no man."

"You cant buy no feed from me, boy," I says. "And if he can eat that loft clean, I'll help you load the barn onto the wagon in the morning."

"He aint never been beholden to no man," he says. "I rather pay you for it."

And if I had my rathers, you wouldn't be here a-tall, I wanted to say. But I just says, "Then it's high time he commenced. You cant buy no feed from me."

When Rachel put supper on, her and the girl went and fixed some beds. But wouldn't any of them come in. "She's been dead long enough to get over that sort of foolishness," I says. Because I got just as much respect for the dead as ere a man, but you've got to respect the dead themselves, and a woman that's been dead in a box four days, the best way to respect her is to get her into the ground as quick as you can. But they wouldn't do it.

"It wouldn't be right," Bundren says. "Course, if the boys wants to go to bed, I reckon I can set up with her. I dont begrudge her it."

So when I went back down there they were squatting on the ground around the wagon, all of them. "Let that chap come to the house and get some sleep, anyway," I says. "And you better come too," I says to the girl. I wasn't aiming to interfere with them. And I sholy hadn't done nothing to her that I knowed.

"He's done already asleep," Bundren says. They had done put him to bed in the trough in a empty stall.

"Well, you come on, then," I says to her. But still she never said nothing. They just squatted there. You couldn't hardly see them. "How about you boys?" I says. "You got a full day tomorrow." After a while Cash says,

"I thank you. We can make out."

"We wouldn't be beholden," Bundren says. "I thank you kindly."

So I left them squatting there. I reckon after four days they was used to it. But Rachel wasn't.

"It's a outrage," she says. "A outrage."

"What could he a done?" I says. "He give her his promised word."

"Who's talking about him?" she says. "Who cares about him?" she says, crying. "I just wish that you and him and all the men in the world that torture us alive and flout us dead, dragging us up and down the country—"

"Now, now," I says. "You're upset."

"Dont you touch me!" she says. "Dont you touch me!"

A man cant tell nothing about them. I lived with the same one fifteen years and I be durn if I can. And I imagined a lot of things coming up between us, but I be durn if I ever thought it would be a body four days dead and that a woman. But they make life hard on them, not taking it as it comes up, like a man does.

So I laid there, hearing it commence to rain, thinking about them down there, squatting around the wagon and the rain on the roof, and thinking about Rachel crying there until after a while it was like I could still hear her crying even after she was asleep, and smelling it even when I knowed I couldn't. I couldn't decide even then whether I could or not, or if it wasn't just knowing it was what it was.

So next morning I never went down there. I heard them hitching up and then when I knowed they must be about ready to take out, I went out the front and went down the road toward the bridge until I heard the wagon come out of the lot and go back toward New Hope. And then when I come back to the house, Rachel jumped on me because I wasn't there to make them come in to breakfast. You cant tell about them. Just about when you decide they mean one thing, I be durn if you not only haven't got to change your mind, like as not you got to take a rawhiding for thinking they meant it.

But it was still like I could smell it. And so I decided then that it wasn't smelling it, but it was just knowing it was there, like you will get fooled now and then. But when I went to the barn I knew different. When I walked into the hallway I saw something. It kind of hunkered up when I come in and I thought at first it was one of them got left, then I saw what it was. It was a buzzard. It looked around and saw me and went on down the hall, spraddle-legged, with its wings kind of hunkered out, watching me first over one shoulder and then over the other, like a old bald-headed man. When it got outdoors it begun to fly. It had to fly a long time before it ever got up into the air, with it thick and heavy and full of rain like it was.

If they was bent on going to Jefferson, I reckon they could have gone around up by Mount Vernon, like MacCallum did. He'll get home about day after tomorrow, horseback. Then they'd be just eighteen

miles from town. But maybe this bridge being gone
too has learned him the Lord's sense and judgment.

That MacCallum. He's been trading with me off and
on for twelve years. I have known him from a boy up;
know his name as well as I do my own. But be durn
if I can say it.

Dewey Dell

(30)

The signboard comes in sight. It is looking out at the road now, because it can wait. New Hope. 3 mi. it will say. New Hope. 3 mi. New Hope. 3 mi. And then the road will begin, curving away into the trees, empty with waiting, saying New Hope three miles.

I heard that my mother is dead. I wish I had time to let her die. I wish I had time to wish I had. It is because in the wild and outraged earth too soon too soon too soon. It's not that I wouldn't and will not it's that it is too soon too soon too soon.

Now it begins to say it. New Hope three miles. New Hope three miles. *That's what they mean by the womb of time: the agony and the despair of spreading bones, the hard girdle in which lie the out-*

raged entrails of events   Cash's head turns slo
as we approach, his pale empty sad composed an .
questioning face following the red and empty curve;
beside the back wheel Jewel sits the horse, gazing
straight ahead.

The land runs out of Darl's eyes; they swim to pin-
points. They begin at my feet and rise along my body
to my face, and then my dress is gone: I sit naked
on the seat above the unhurrying mules, above the
travail. *Suppose I tell him to turn. He will do what
I say. Dont you know he will do what I say?* Once I
waked with a black void rushing under me. I could
not see. I saw Vardaman rise and go to the window
and strike the knife into the fish, the blood gushing,
hissing like steam but I could not see. *He'll do as I
say. He always does. I can persuade him to anything.
You know I can. Suppose I say Turn here.* That was
when I died that time. *Suppose I do. We'll go to New
Hope. We wont have to go to town.*   I rose and
took the knife from the streaming fish still hissing and
I killed Darl.

*When I used to sleep with Vardaman I had a night-
mare once I thought I was awake but I couldn't see
and couldn't feel I couldn't feel the bed under me and
I couldn't think what I was I couldn't think of my
name I couldn't even think I am a girl I couldn't even
think I nor even think I want to wake up nor remember what was opposite to awake so I could do that
I knew that something was passing but I couldn't
even think of time then all of a sudden I knew that
something was it was wind blowing over me it was
like the wind came and blew me back from where it
was I was not blowing the room and Vardaman asleep
and all of them back under me again and going on*

like a piece of cool silk dragging across my naked legs

It blows cool out of the pines, a sad steady sound. New Hope. Was 3 mi. Was 3 mi. I believe in God I believe in God.

"Why didn't we go to New Hope, pa?" Vardaman says. "Mr Samson said we was, but we done passed the road."

Darl says, "Look, Jewel." But he is not looking at me. He is looking at the sky. The buzzard is as still as if he were nailed to it.

We turn into Tull's lane. We pass the barn and go on, the wheels whispering in the mud, passing the green rows of cotton in the wild earth, and Vernon little across the field behind the plow. He lifts his hand as we pass and stands there looking after us for a long while.

"Look, Jewel," Darl says. Jewel sits on his horse like they were both made out of wood, looking straight ahead.

I believe in God, God. God, I believe in God.

Tull

After they passed I taken the mule out and looped up
the trace chains and followed. They was setting in
the wagon at the end of the levee when I caught up
with them. Anse was setting there, looking at the
bridge where it was swagged down into the river with
just the two ends in sight. He was looking at it like
he had believed all the time that folks had been lying
to him about it being gone, but like he was hoping
all the time it really was. Kind of pleased astonishment
he looked, setting on the wagon in his Sunday pants,
mumbling his mouth. Looking like a uncurried horse
dressed up: I dont know.

The boy was watching the bridge where it was
mid-sunk and logs and such drifted up over it and it

swagging and shivering like the whole thing would
go any minute, big-eyed he was watching it, like he
was to a circus. And the gal too. When I come up she
looked around at me, her eyes kind of blaring up and
going hard like I had made to touch her. Then she
looked at Anse again and then back at the water
again.

It was nigh up to the levee on both sides, the earth
hid except for the tongue of it we was on going out to
the bridge and then down into the water, and except
for knowing how the road and the bridge used to
look, a fellow couldn't tell where was the river and
where the land. It was just a tangle of yellow and the
levee not less wider than a knife-back kind of, with
us setting in the wagon and on the horse and the mule.

Darl was looking at me, and then Cash turned and
looked at me with that look in his eyes like when he
was figuring on whether the planks would fit her that
night, like he was measuring them inside of him and
not asking you to say what you thought and not even
letting on he was listening if you did say it, but listening all right. Jewel hadn't moved. He sat there on the
horse, leaning a little forward, with that same look
on his face when him and Darl passed the house yesterday, coming back to get her.

"If it was just up, we could drive across," Anse says.
"We could drive right on across it."

Sometimes a log would get shoved over the jam and
float on, rolling and turning, and we could watch it
go on to where the ford used to be. It would slow up
and whirl crossways and hang out of water for a
minute, and you could tell by that that the ford used
to be there.

"But that dont show nothing," I say. "It could be

a bar of quicksand built up there." We watch the log.
Then the gal is looking at me again.

"Mr Whitfield crossed it," she says.

"He was a-horseback," I say. "And three days ago.
It's riz five foot since."

"If the bridge was just up," Anse says.

The log bobs up and goes on again. There is a lot
of trash and foam, and you can hear the water.

"But it's down," Anse says.

Cash says, "A careful fellow could walk across
yonder on the planks and logs."

"But you couldn't tote nothing," I say. "Likely time
you set foot on that mess, it'll all go, too. What you
think, Darl?"

He is looking at me. He dont say nothing; just
looks at me with them queer eyes of hisn that makes
folks talk. I always say it aint never been what he
done so much or said or anything so much as how he
looks at you. It's like he had got into the inside of you,
someway. Like somehow you was looking at yourself
and your doings outen his eyes. Then I can feel that
gal watching me like I had made to touch her. She
says something to Anse. ". . . Mr Whitfield . . ."
she says.

"I give her my promised word in the presence of
the Lord," Anse says. "I reckon it aint no need to
worry."

But still he does not start the mules. We set there
above the water. Another log bobs up over the jam
and goes on; we watch it check up and swing slow for
a minute where the ford used to be. Then it goes on.

"It might start falling tonight," I say. "You could
lay over one more day."

Then Jewel turns sideways on the horse. He has

not moved until then, and he turns and looks at me.
His face is kind of green, then it would go red and
then green again. "Get to hell on back to your damn
plowing," he says. "Who the hell asked you to follow
us here?"

"I never meant no harm," I say.

"Shut up, Jewel," Cash says. Jewel looks back at
the water, his face gritted, going red and green and
then red. "Well," Cash says after a while, "what you
want to do?"

Anse dont say nothing. He sets humped up, mumbling his mouth. "If it was just up, we could drive
across it," he says.

"Come on," Jewel says, moving the horse.

"Wait," Cash says. He looks at the bridge. We look
at him, except Anse and the gal. They are looking at
the water. "Dewey Dell and Vardaman and pa better
walk across on the bridge," Cash says.

"Vernon can help them," Jewel says. "And we can
hitch his mule ahead of ourn."

"You aint going to take my mule into that water,"
I say.

Jewel looks at me. His eyes look like pieces of a
broken plate. "I'll pay for your damn mule. I'll buy
it from you right now."

"My mule aint going into that water," I say.

"Jewel's going to use his horse," Darl says. "Why
wont you risk your mule, Vernon?"

"Shut up, Darl," Cash says. "You and Jewel both."

"My mule aint going into that water," I say.

Darl

He sits the horse, glaring at Vernon, his lean face
suffused up to and beyond the pale rigidity of his eyes.
The summer when he was fifteen, he took a spell of
sleeping. One morning when I went to feed the mules
the cows were still in the tie-up and then I heard pa
go back to the house and call him. When we came
on back to the house for breakfast he passed us, carrying the milk buckets, stumbling along like he was
drunk, and he was milking when we put the mules in
and went on to the field without him. We had been
there an hour and still he never showed up. When
Dewey Dell came with our lunch, pa sent her back
to find Jewel. They found him in the tie-up, sitting
on the stool, asleep.

After that, every morning pa would go in and wake him. He would go to sleep at the supper table and soon as supper was finished he would go to bed, and when I came in to bed he would be lying there like a dead man. Yet still pa would have to wake him in the morning. He would get up, but he wouldn't hardly have half sense: he would stand for pa's jawing and complaining without a word and take the milk buckets and go to the barn, and once I found him asleep at the cow, the bucket in place and half full and his hands up to the wrists in the milk and his head against the cow's flank.

After that Dewey Dell had to do the milking. He still got up when pa waked him, going about what we told him to do in that dazed way. It was like he was trying hard to do them; that he was as puzzled as anyone else.

"Are you sick?" ma said. "Dont you feel all right?"

"Yes," Jewel said. "I feel all right."

"He's just lazy, trying me," pa said, and Jewel standing there, asleep on his feet like as not. "Aint you?" he said, waking Jewel up again to answer.

"No," Jewel said.

"You take off and stay in the house today," ma said.

"With that whole bottom piece to be busted out?" pa said. "If you aint sick, what's the matter with you?"

"Nothing," Jewel said. "I'm all right."

"All right?" pa said. "You're asleep on your feet this minute."

"No," Jewel said. "I'm all right."

"I want him to stay at home today," ma said.

"I'll need him," pa said. "It's tight enough, with all of us to do it."

"You'll just have to do the best you can with Cash and Darl," ma said. "I want him to stay in today."

But he wouldn't do it. "I'm all right," he said, going on. But he wasn't all right. Anybody could see it. He was losing flesh, and I have seen him go to sleep chopping: watched the hoe going slower and slower up and down, with less and less of an arc, until it stopped and he leaning on it motionless in the hot shimmer of the sun.

Ma wanted to get the doctor, but pa didn't want to spend the money without it was needful, and Jewel did seem all right except for his thinness and his way of dropping off to sleep at any moment. He ate hearty enough, except for his way of going to sleep in his plate, with a piece of bread halfway to his mouth and his jaws still chewing. But he swore he was all right.

It was ma that got Dewey Dell to do his milking, paid her somehow, and the other jobs around the house that Jewel had been doing before supper she found some way for Dewey Dell and Vardaman to do them. And doing them herself when pa wasn't there. She would fix him special things to eat and hide them for him. And that may have been when I first found it out, that Addie Bundren should be hiding anything she did, who had tried to teach us that deceit was such that, in a world where it was, nothing else could be very bad or very important, not even poverty. And at times when I went in to go to bed she would be sitting in the dark by Jewel where he was asleep. And I knew that she was hating herself for that deceit and hating Jewel because she had to love him so that she had to act the deceit.

One night she was taken sick and when I went to

the barn to put the team in and drive to Tull's, I couldn't find the lantern. I remembered noticing it on the nail the night before, but it wasn't there now at midnight. So I hitched in the dark and went on and came back with Mrs Tull just after daylight. And there the lantern was, hanging on the nail where I remembered it and couldn't find it before. And then one morning while Dewey Dell was milking just before sunup, Jewel came into the barn from the back, through the hole in the back wall, with the lantern in his hand.

I told Cash, and Cash and I looked at one another.

"Rutting," Cash said.

"Yes," I said. "But why the lantern? And every night, too. No wonder he's losing flesh. Are you going to say anything to him?"

"Wont do any good," Cash said.

"What he's doing now wont do any good, either."

"I know. But he'll have to learn that himself. Give him time to realise that it'll save, that there'll be just as much more tomorrow, and he'll be all right. I wouldn't tell anybody, I reckon."

"No," I said. "I told Dewey Dell not to. Not ma, anyway."

"No. Not ma."

After that I thought it was right comical: he acting so bewildered and willing and dead for sleep and gaunt as a bean-pole, and thinking he was so smart with it. And I wondered who the girl was. I thought of all I knew that it might be, but I couldn't say for sure.

" 'Taint any girl," Cash said. "It's a married woman somewhere. Aint any young girl got that much daring and staying power. That's what I dont like about it."

"Why?" I said. "She'll be safer for him than a girl would. More judgment."

He looked at me, his eyes fumbling, the words fumbling at what he was trying to say. "It aint always the safe things in this world that a fellow . . ."

"You mean, the safe things are not always the best things?"

"Ay; best," he said, fumbling again. "It aint the best things, the things that are good for him . . . A young boy. A fellow kind of hates to see . . . wallowing in somebody else's mire . . ." That's what he was trying to say. When something is new and hard and bright, there ought to be something a little better for it than just being safe, since the safe things are just the things that folks have been doing so long they have worn the edges off and there's nothing to the doing of them that leaves a man to say, That was not done before and it cannot be done again.

So we didn't tell, not even when after a while he'd appear suddenly in the field beside us and go to work, without having had time to get home and make out he had been in bed all night. He would tell ma that he hadn't been hungry at breakfast or that he had eaten a piece of bread while he was hitching up the team. But Cash and I knew that he hadn't been home at all on those nights and he had come up out of the woods when we got to the field. But we didn't tell. Summer was almost over then; we knew that when the nights began to get cool, she would be done if he wasn't.

But when fall came and the nights began to get longer, the only difference was that he would always be in bed for pa to wake him, getting him up at last in that first state of semi-idiocy like when it first started, worse than when he had stayed out all night.

"She's sure a stayer," I told Cash. "I used to admire her, but I downright respect her now."

"It aint a woman," he said.

"You know," I said. But he was watching me. "What is it, then?"

"That's what I aim to find out," he said.

"You can trail him through the woods all night if you want to," I said. "I'm not."

"I aint trailing him," he said.

"What do you call it, then?"

"I aint trailing him," he said. "I dont mean it that way."

And so a few nights later I heard Jewel get up and climb out the window, and then I heard Cash get up and follow him. The next morning when I went to the barn, Cash was already there, the mules fed, and he was helping Dewey Dell milk. And when I saw him I knew that he knew what it was. Now and then I would catch him watching Jewel with a queer look, like having found out where Jewel went and what he was doing had given him something to really think about at last. But it was not a worried look; it was the kind of look I would see on him when I would find him doing some of Jewel's work around the house, work that pa still thought Jewel was doing and that ma thought Dewey Dell was doing. So I said nothing to him, believing that when he got done digesting it in his mind, he would tell me. But he never did.

One morning—it was November then, five months since it started—Jewel was not in bed and he didn't join us in the field. That was the first time ma learned anything about what had been going on. She sent Vardaman down to find where Jewel was, and after

a while she came down too. It was as though, so long
as the deceit ran along quiet and monotonous, all of
us let ourselves be deceived, abetting it unawares or
maybe through cowardice, since all people are cow-
ards and naturally prefer any kind of treachery because it has a bland outside. But now it was like we
had all—and by a kind of telepathic agreement of
admitted fear—flung the whole thing back like covers
on the bed and we all sitting bolt upright in our
nakedness, staring at one another and saying "Now
is the truth. He hasn't come home. Something has
happened to him. We let something happen to him."

Then we saw him. He came up along the ditch and
then turned straight across the field, riding the horse.
Its mane and tail were going, as though in motion they
were carrying out the splotchy pattern of its coat:
he looked like he was riding on a big pinwheel, bare-
backed, with a rope bridle, and no hat on his head.
It was a descendant of those Texas ponies Flem
Snopes brought here twenty-five years ago and auc-
tioned off for two dollars a head and nobody but old
Lon Quick ever caught his and still owned some of
the blood because he could never give it away.

He galloped up and stopped, his heels in the horse's
ribs and it dancing and swirling like the shape of its
mane and tail and the splotches of its coat had nothing whatever to do with the flesh-and-bone horse inside them, and he sat there, looking at us.

"Where did you get that horse?" pa said.

"Bought it," Jewel said. "From Mr Quick."

"Bought it?" pa said. "With what? Did you buy
that thing on my word?"

"It was my money," Jewel said. "I earned it. You
wont need to worry about it."

"Jewel," ma said; "Jewel."

"It's all right," Cash said. "He earned the money. He cleaned up that forty acres of new ground Quick laid out last spring. He did it single handed, working at night by lantern. I saw him. So I dont reckon that horse cost anybody anything except Jewel. I dont reckon we need worry."

"Jewel," ma said. "Jewel . . ." Then she said: "You come right to the house and go to bed."

"Not yet," Jewel said. "I aint got time. I got to get me a saddle and bridle. Mr Quick says he . . ."

"Jewel," ma said, looking at him. "I'll give—I'll give . . . give . . ." Then she began to cry. She cried hard, not hiding her face, standing there in her faded wrapper, looking at him and him on the horse, looking down at her, his face growing cold and a little sick looking, until he looked away quick and Cash came and touched her.

"You go on to the house," Cash said. "This here ground is too wet for you. You go on, now." She put her hands to her face then and after a while she went on, stumbling a little on the plow-marks. But pretty soon she straightened up and went on. She didn't look back. When she reached the ditch she stopped and called Vardaman. He was looking at the horse, kind of dancing up and down by it.

"Let me ride, Jewel," he said. "Let me ride, Jewel."

Jewel looked at him, then he looked away again, holding the horse reined back. Pa watched him, mumbling his lip.

"So you bought a horse," he said. "You went behind my back and bought a horse. You never consulted me; you know how tight it is for us to make by, yet you bought a horse for me to feed. Taken the work from your flesh and blood and bought a horse with it."

Jewel looked at pa, his eyes paler than ever. "He wont never eat a mouthful of yours," he said. "Not a mouthful. I'll kill him first. Dont you never think it. Dont you never."

"Let me ride, Jewel," Vardaman said. "Let me ride, Jewel." He sounded like a cricket in the grass, a little one. "Let me ride, Jewel."

That night I found ma sitting beside the bed where he was sleeping, in the dark. She cried hard, maybe because she had to cry so quiet; maybe because she felt the same way about tears she did about deceit, hating herself for doing it, hating him because she had to. And then I knew that I knew. I knew that as plain on that day as I knew about Dewey Dell on that day.

Tull

So they finally got Anse to say what he wanted to do, and him and the gal and the boy got out of the wagon. But even when we were on the bridge Anse kept on looking back, like he thought maybe, once he was outen the wagon, the whole thing would kind of blow up and he would find himself back yonder in the field again and her laying up there in the house, waiting to die and it to do all over again.

"You ought to let them taken your mule," he says, and the bridge shaking and swaying under us, going down into the moiling water like it went clean through to the other side of the earth, and the other end coming up outen the water like it wasn't the same bridge a-tall and that them that would walk up outen the water on that side must come from the bottom of the earth. But it was still whole; you could tell that by the way when this end swagged, it didn't look like the other end swagged at all: just like the other trees and the bank yonder were swinging back and forth slow like on a big clock. And them logs scraping and bumping at the sunk part and tilting end-up and shooting clean outen the water and tumbling on toward the ford and the waiting, slick, whirling, and foamy.

"What good would that a done?" I says. "If your team cant find the ford and haul it across, what good would three mules or even ten mules do?"

"I aint asking it of you," he says. "I can always do for me and mine. I aint asking you to risk your mule. It aint your dead; I am not blaming you."

"They ought to went back and laid over until tomorrow," I says. The water was cold. It was thick, like slush ice. Only it kind of lived. One part of you knowed it was just water, the same thing that had been running under this same bridge for a long time, yet when them logs would come spewing up outen it, you were not surprised, like they was a part of water, of the waiting and the threat.

It was like when we was across, up out of the water again and the hard earth under us, that I was surprised. It was like we hadn't expected the bridge to end on the other bank, on something tame like the hard earth again that we had tromped on before this time and knowed well. Like it couldn't be me here, because I'd have had better sense than to done what I just done. And when I looked back and saw the other bank and saw my mule standing there where I used to be and knew that I'd have to get back there someway, I knew it couldn't be, because I just couldn't think of anything that could make me cross that bridge ever even once. Yet here I was, and the fellow that could make himself cross it twice, couldn't be me, not even if Cora told him to.

It was that boy. I said "Here; you better take a holt of my hand" and he waited and held to me. I be durn if it wasn't like he come back and got me; like he was saying They wont nothing hurt you. Like he was saying about a fine place he knowed where Christmas come twice with Thanksgiving and lasts on through the winter and the spring and the summer, and if I just stayed with him I'd be all right too.

When I looked back at my mule it was like he was one of these here spy-glasses and I could look at him standing there and see all the broad land and my house sweated outen it like it was the more the sweat, the broader the land; the more the sweat, the tighter the house because it would take a tight house for Cora, to hold Cora like a jar of milk in the spring: you've got to have a tight jar or you'll need a powerful spring, so if you have a big spring, why then you have the incentive to have tight, wellmade jars, because it is your milk, sour or not, because you would rather have milk that will sour than to have milk that wont, because you are a man.

And him holding to my hand, his hand that hot and confident, so that I was like to say: Look-a-here. Cant you see that mule yonder? He never had no business over here, so he never come, not being nothing but a mule. Because a fellow can see ever now and then that children have more sense than him. But he dont like to admit it to them until they have beards. After they have a beard, they are too busy because they dont know if they'll ever quite make it back to where they were in sense before they was haired, so you dont mind admitting then to folks that are worrying about the same thing that aint worth the worry that you are yourself.

Then we was over and we stood there, looking at Cash turning the wagon around. We watched them drive back down the road to where the trail turned off into the bottom. After a while the wagon was out of sight.

"We better get on down to the ford and git ready to help," I said.

"I give her my word," Anse says. "It is sacred on me. I know you begrudge it, but she will bless you in heaven."

"Well, they got to finish circumventing the land before they can dare the water," I said. "Come on."

"It's the turning back," he said. "It aint no luck in turning back."

He was standing there, humped, mournful, looking at the empty road beyond the swagging and swaying bridge. And that gal, too, with the lunch basket on one arm and that package under the other. Just going to town. Bent on it. They would risk the fire and the earth and the water and all just to eat a sack of bananas. "You ought to laid over a day," I said. "It would a fell some by morning. It mought not a rained tonight. And it cant get no higher."

"I give my promise," he says. "She is counting on it."

Darl

Before us the thick dark current runs. It talks up to us in a murmur become ceaseless and myriad, the yellow surface dimpled monstrously into fading swirls travelling along the surface for an instant, silent, impermanent and profoundly significant, as though just beneath the surface something huge and alive waked for a moment of lazy alertness out of and into light slumber again.

It clucks and murmurs among the spokes and about the mules' knees, yellow, skummed with flotsam and with thick soiled gouts of foam as though it had sweat, lathering, like a driven horse. Through the undergrowth it goes with a plaintive sound, a musing sound; in it the unwinded cane and saplings lean as before a little gale, swaying without reflections as though suspended on invisible wires from the branches overhead. Above the ceaseless surface they stand—trees, cane, vines—rootless, severed from the earth, spectral above a scene of immense yet circumscribed desolation filled with the voice of the waste and mournful water.

Cash and I sit in the wagon; Jewel sits the horse at the off rear wheel. The horse is trembling, its eye rolling wild and baby-blue in its long pink face, its breathing stertorous like groaning. He sits erect, poised, looking quietly and steadily and quickly this way and that, his face calm, a little pale, alert. Cash's face is also gravely composed; he and I look at one another with long probing looks, looks that plunge unimpeded through one another's eyes and into the ultimate secret place where for an instant Cash and Darl crouch flagrant and unabashed in all the old terror and the old foreboding, alert and secret and without shame. When we speak our voices are quiet, detached.

"I reckon we're still in the road, all right."

"Tull taken and cut them two big whiteoaks. I heard tell how at high water in the old days they used to line up the ford by them trees."

"I reckon he did that two years ago when he was logging down here. I reckon he never thought that anybody would ever use this ford again."

"I reckon not. Yes, it must have been then. He cut a sight of timber outen here then. Payed off that mortgage with it, I hear tell."

"Yes. Yes, I reckon so. I reckon Vernon could have done that."

"That's a fact. Most folks that logs in this here

country, they need a durn good farm to support the sawmill. Or maybe a store. But I reckon Vernon could."

"I reckon so. He's a sight."

"Ay. Vernon is. Yes, it must still be here. He never would have got that timber out of here if he hadn't cleaned out that old road. I reckon we are still on it." He looks about quietly, at the position of the trees, leaning this way and that, looking back along the floorless road shaped vaguely high in air by the position of the lopped and felled trees, as if the road too had been soaked free of earth and floated upward, to leave in its spectral tracing a monument to a still more profound desolation than this above which we now sit, talking quietly of old security and old trivial things. Jewel looks at him, then at me, then his face turns in in that quiet, constant, questing about the scene, the horse trembling quietly and steadily between his knees.

"He could go on ahead slow and sort of feel it out," I say.

"Yes," Cash says, not looking at me. His face is in profile as he looks forward where Jewel has moved on ahead.

"He cant miss the river," I say. "He couldn't miss seeing it fifty yards ahead."

Cash does not look at me, his face in profile. "If I'd just suspicioned it, I could a come down last week and taken a sight on it."

"The bridge was up then," I say. He does not look at me. "Whitfield crossed it a-horseback."

Jewel looks at us again, his expression sober and alert and subdued. His voice is quiet. "What you want me to do?"

"I ought to come down last week and taken a sight on it," Cash says.

"We couldn't have known," I say. "There wasn't any way for us to know."

"I'll ride on ahead," Jewel says. "You can follow where I am." He lifts the horse. It shrinks, bowed; he leans to it, speaking to it, lifting it forward almost bodily, it setting its feet down with gingerly splashings, trembling, breathing harshly. He speaks to it, murmurs to it. "Go on," he says. "I aint going to let nothing hurt you. Go on, now."

"Jewel," Cash says. Jewel does not look back. He lifts the horse on.

"He can swim," I say. "If he'll just give the horse time, anyhow . . ." When he was born, he had a bad time of it. Ma would sit in the lamp-light, holding him on a pillow on her lap. We would wake and find her so. There would be no sound from them.

"That pillow was longer than him," Cash says. He is leaning a little forward. "I ought to come down last week and sighted. I ought to done it."

"That's right," I say. "Neither his feet nor his head would reach the end of it. You couldn't have known," I say.

"I ought to done it," he says. He lifts the reins. The mules move, into the traces; the wheels murmur alive in the water. He looks back and down at Addie. "It aint on a balance," he says.

At last the trees open; against the open river Jewel sits the horse, half turned, it belly deep now. Across the river we can see Vernon and pa and Vardaman and Dewey Dell. Vernon is waving at us, waving us further downstream.

"We are too high up," Cash says. Vernon is shouting too, but we cannot make out what he says for the noise of the water. It runs steady and deep now, unbroken, without sense of motion until a log comes along, turning slowly. "Watch it," Cash says. We watch it and see it falter and hang for a moment, the current building up behind it in a thick wave, submerging it for an instant before it shoots up and tumbles on.

"There it is," I say.

"Ay," Cash says. "It's there." We look at Vernon again. He is now flapping his arms up and down. We move on downstream, slowly and carefully, watching Vernon. He drops his hands. "This is the place," Cash says.

"Well, goddamn it, let's get across, then," Jewel says. He moves the horse on.

"You wait," Cash says. Jewel stops again.

"Well, by God—" he says. Cash looks at the water, then he looks back at Addie. "It aint on a balance," he says.

"Then go on back to the goddamn bridge and walk across," Jewel says. "You and Darl both. Let me on that wagon."

Cash does not pay him any attention. "It aint on a balance," he says. "Yes, sir. We got to watch it."

"Watch it, hell," Jewel says. "You get out of that wagon and let me have it. By God, if you're afraid to drive it over . . ." His eyes are pale as two bleached chips in his face. Cash is looking at him.

"We'll get it over," he says. "I tell you what you do. You ride on back and walk across the bridge and come down the other bank and meet us with the rope. Vernon'll take your horse home with him and keep it till we get back."

"You go to hell," Jewel says.

"You take the rope and come down the bank and be ready with it," Cash says. "Three cant do no more than two can—one to drive and one to steady it."

"Goddamn you," Jewel says.

"Let Jewel take the end of the rope and cross upstream of us and brace it," I say. "Will you do that, Jewel?"

Jewel watches me, hard. He looks quick at Cash, then back at me, his eyes alert and hard. "I dont give a damn. Just so we do something. Setting here, not lifting a goddamn hand . . ."

"Let's do that, Cash," I say.

"I reckon we'll have to," Cash says.

The river itself is not a hundred yards across, and pa and Vernon and Vardaman and Dewey Dell are the only things in sight not of that single monotony of desolation leaning with that terrific quality a little from right to left, as though we had reached the place where the motion of the wasted world accelerates just before the final precipice. Yet they appear dwarfed. It is as though the space between us were time: an irrevocable quality. It is as though time, no longer running straight before us in a diminishing line, now runs parallel between us like a looping string, the distance being the doubling accretion of the thread and not the interval between. The mules stand, their fore quarters already sloped a little, their rumps high. They too are breathing now with a deep groaning sound; looking back once, their gaze sweeps across us with in their eyes a wild, sad, profound and despairing quality as though they had already seen in the thick water the shape of the disaster which they could not speak and we could not see.

Cash turns back into the wagon. He lays his hands flat on Addie, rocking her a little. His face is calm, down-sloped, calculant, concerned. He lifts his box of tools and wedges it forward under the seat; together we shove Addie forward, wedging her between the tools and the wagon bed. Then he looks at me.

"No," I say. "I reckon I'll stay. Might take both of us."

From the tool box he takes his coiled rope and carries the end twice around the seat stanchion and passes the end to me without tying it. The other end he pays out to Jewel, who takes a turn about his saddle horn.

He must force the horse down into the current. It moves, highkneed, archnecked, boring and chafing. Jewel sits lightly forward, his knees lifted a little; again his swift alert calm gaze sweeps upon us and on. He lowers the horse into the stream, speaking to it in a soothing murmur. The horse slips, goes under to the saddle, surges to its feet again, the current building up against Jewel's thighs.

"Watch yourself," Cash says.

"I'm on it now," Jewel says. "You can come ahead now."

Cash takes the reins and lowers the team carefully and skillfully into the stream.

I felt the current take us and I knew we were on the ford by that reason, since it was only by means of that slipping contact that we could tell that we were in motion at all. What had once been a flat surface was now a succession of troughs and hillocks lifting and falling about us, shoving at us, teasing at us with light lazy touches in the vain instants of solidity underfoot. Cash looked back at me, and then I knew that we were gone. But I did not realise the reason for the rope until I saw the log. It surged up out of the water and stood for an instant upright upon that surging and heaving desolation like Christ. Get out and let the current take you down to the bend, Cash said. You can make it all right. No, I said, I'd get just as wet that way as this

The log appears suddenly between two hills, as if it had rocketed suddenly from the bottom of the river. Upon the end of it a long gout of foam hangs like the beard of an old man or a goat. When Cash speaks to me I know that he has been watching it all the time, watching it and watching Jewel ten feet ahead of us. "Let the rope go," he says. With his other hand he reaches down and reeves the two turns from the stanchion. "Ride on, Jewel," he says; "see if you can pull us ahead of the log."

Jewel shouts at the horse; again he appears to lift it bodily between his knees. He is just above the top of the ford and the horse has a purchase of some sort for it surges forward, shining wetly half out of water, crashing on in a succession of lunges. It moves unbelievably fast; by that token Jewel realises at last that the rope is free, for I can see him sawing back on the reins, his head turned, as the log rears in a long sluggish lunge between us, bearing down upon the team. They see it too; for a moment they also shine black out of water. Then the downstream one vanishes, dragging the other with him; the wagon sheers crosswise, poised on the crest of the ford as the log strikes it, tilting it up and on. Cash is half turned, the reins running taut from his hand and disappearing into the water, the other hand reached back upon Addie, holding her jammed over against the

high side of the wagon. "Jump clear," he says quietly.
"Stay away from the team and dont try to fight it.
It'll swing you into the bend all right."

"You come too," I say. Vernon and Vardaman are
running along the bank, pa and Dewey Dell stand
watching us, Dewey Dell with the basket and the
package in her arms. Jewel is trying to fight the horse
back. The head of one mule appears, its eyes wide;
it looks back at us for an instant, making a sound
almost human. The head vanishes again.

"Back, Jewel," Cash shouts. "Back, Jewel." For another instant I see him leaning to the tilting wagon,
his arm braced back against Addie and his tools; I
see the bearded head of the rearing log strike up
again, and beyond it Jewel holding the horse upreared, its head wrenched around, hammering its
head with his fist. I jump from the wagon on the
downstream side. Between two hills I see the mules
once more. They roll up out of the water in succession, turning completely over, their legs stiffly extended as when they had lost contact with the earth.

Vardaman

Cash tried but she fell off and Darl jumped going under he went under and Cash hollering to catch her and I hollering running and hollering and Dewey Dell hollering at me Vardaman you vardaman you vardaman and Vernon passed me because he was seeing her come up and she jumped into the water again and Darl hadn't caught her yet

He came up to see and I hollering catch her Darl catch her and he didn't come back because she was too heavy he had to go on catching at her and I hollering catch her darl catch her darl because in the water she could go faster than a man and Darl had to grabble for her so I knew he could catch her because he is the best grabbler even with the mules in the way again they dived up rolling their feet stiff rolling down again and their backs up now and Darl had to again because in the water she could go faster than a man or woman and I passed Vernon and he wouldn't get in the water and help Darl he wouldn't grabble for her with Darl he knew but he wouldn't help

The mules dived up again diving their legs stiff their stiff legs rolling slow and then Darl again and I hollering catch her darl catch her head her into the bank darl and Vernon wouldn't help and then Darl dodged past the mules where he could he had her under the water coming in to the bank coming in slow because in the water she fought to stay under the water but Darl is strong and he was coming in slow and so I knew he had her because he came slow and I ran down into the water to help and I couldn't stop hollering because Darl was strong and steady holding her under the water even if she did fight he would not let her go he was seeing me and he would hold her and it was all right now it was all right now it was all right

Then he comes up out of the water. He comes a long way up slow before his hands do but he's got to have her got to so I can bear it. Then his hands come up and all of him above the water. I cant stop. I have not got time to try. I will try to when I can but his hands came empty out of the water emptying the water emptying away

"Where is ma, Darl?" I said. "You never got her. You knew she is a fish but you let her get away. You never got her. Darl. Darl. Darl." I began to run along the bank, watching the mules dive up slow again and then down again.

Tull

When I told Cora how Darl jumped out of the wagon and left Cash sitting there trying to save it and the wagon turning over, and Jewel that was almost to the bank fighting that horse back where it had more sense than to go, she says "And you're one of the folks that says Darl is the queer one, the one that aint bright, and him the only one of them that had sense enough to get off that wagon. I notice Anse was too smart to been on it a-tall."

"He couldn't a done no good, if he'd been there," I said. "They was going about it right and they would have made it if it hadn't a been for that log."

"Log, fiddlesticks," Cora said. "It was the hand of God."

"Then how can you say it was foolish?" I said. "Nobody cant guard against the hand of God. It would be sacrilege to try to."

"Then why dare it?" Cora says. "Tell me that."

"Anse didn't," I said. "That's just what you faulted him for."

"His place was there," Cora said. "If he had been a man, he would a been there instead of making his sons do what he dursn't."

"I dont know what you want, then," I said. "One breath you say they was daring the hand of God to try it, and the next breath you jump on Anse because he wasn't with them." Then she begun to sing again, working at the washtub, with that singing look in her face like she had done give up folks and all their foolishness and had done went on ahead of them, marching up the sky, singing.

The wagon hung for a long time while the current built up under it, shoving it off the ford, and Cash leaning more and more, trying to keep the coffin braced so it wouldn't slip down and finish tilting the wagon over. Soon as the wagon got tilted good, to where the current could finish it, the log went on. It headed around the wagon and went on good as a swimming man could have done. It was like it had been sent there to do a job and done it and went on.

When the mules finally kicked loose, it looked for a minute like maybe Cash would get the wagon back. It looked like him and the wagon wasn't moving at all, and just Jewel fighting that horse back to the wagon. Then that boy passed me, running and hollering at Darl and the gal trying to catch him, and then I see the mules come rolling slow up out of the water, their legs spraddled stiff like they had balked upside down, and roll on into the water again.

Then the wagon tilted over and then it and Jewel and the horse was all mixed up together. Cash went outen sight, still holding the coffin braced, and then I couldn't tell anything for the horse lunging and splashing. I thought that Cash had give up then and was swimming for it and I was yelling at Jewel to come on back and then all of a sudden him and the horse went under too and I thought they was all going. I knew that the horse had got dragged off the ford too, and with that wild drowning horse and that wagon and that loose box, it was going to be pretty bad, and there I was, standing knee-deep in the water, yelling at Anse behind me: "See what you done now? See what you done now?"

The horse come up again. It was headed for the bank now, throwing its head up, and then I saw one of them holding to the saddle on the downstream side, so I started running along the bank, trying to catch sight of Cash because he couldn't swim, yelling at Jewel where Cash was like a durn fool, bad as that boy that was on down the bank still hollering at Darl.

So I went down into the water so I could still keep some kind of a grip in the mud, when I saw Jewel. He was middle deep, so I knew he was on the ford, anyway, leaning hard upstream, and then I see the rope, and then I see the water building up where he was holding the wagon snubbed just below the ford.

So it was Cash holding to the horse when it come splashing and scrambling up the bank, moaning and groaning like a natural man. When I come to it it was just kicking Cash loose from his holt on the saddle.

His face turned up a second when he was sliding back into the water. It was gray, with his eyes closed and a long swipe of mud across his face. Then he let go and turned over in the water. He looked just like a old bundle of clothes kind of washing up and down against the bank. He looked like he was laying there in the water on his face, rocking up and down a little, looking at something on the bottom.

We could watch the rope cutting down into the water, and we could feel the weight of the wagon kind of blump and lunge lazy like, like it just as soon as not, and that rope cutting down into the water hard as a iron bar. We could hear the water hissing on it like it was red hot. Like it was a straight iron bar stuck into the bottom and us holding the end of it, and the wagon lazing up and down, kind of pushing and prodding at us like it had come around and got behind us, lazy like, like it just as soon as not when it made up its mind. There was a shoat come by, blowed up like a balloon: one of them spotted shoats of Lon Quick's. It bumped against the rope like it was a iron bar and bumped off and went on, and us watching that rope slanting down into the water. We watched it.

Darl

Cash lies on his back on the earth, his head raised on a rolled garment. His eyes are closed, his face is gray, his hair plastered in a smooth smear across his forehead as though done with a paint brush. His face appears sunken a little, sagging from the bony ridges of eye sockets, nose, gums, as though the wetting had slacked the firmness which had held the skin full; his teeth, set in pale gums, are parted a little as if he had been laughing quietly. He lies pole-thin in his wet clothes, a little pool of vomit at his head and a thread of it running from the corner of his mouth and down his cheek where he couldn't turn his head quick or far enough, until Dewey Dell stoops and wipes it away with the hem of her dress.

Jewel approaches. He has the plane. "Vernon just found the square," he says. He looks down at Cash, dripping too. "Aint he talked none yet?"

"He had his saw and hammer and chalk-line and rule," I say. "I know that."

Jewel lays the square down. Pa watches him. "They cant be far away," pa says. "It all went together. Was there ere a such misfortunate man."

Jewel does not look at pa. "You better call Vardaman back here," he says. He looks at Cash. Then he turns and goes away. "Get him to talk soon as he can," he says, "so he can tell us what else there was."

We return to the river. The wagon is hauled clear, the wheels chocked (carefully: we all helped; it is as though upon the shabby, familiar, inert shape of the wagon there lingered somehow, latent yet still immediate, that violence which had slain the mules that drew it not an hour since) above the edge of the flood. In the wagon bed it lies profoundly, the long pale planks hushed a little with wetting yet still yellow, like gold seen through water, save for two long muddy smears. We pass it and go on to the bank.

One end of the rope is made fast to a tree. At the edge of the stream, knee-deep, Vardaman stands, bent forward a little, watching Vernon with rapt absorption. He has stopped yelling and he is wet to the armpits. Vernon is at the other end of the rope, shoulder-deep in the river, looking back at Vardaman. "Further back than that," he says. "You git back by the tree and hold the rope for me, so it cant slip."

Vardaman backs along the rope, to the tree, moving blindly, watching Vernon. When we come up he looks at us once, his eyes round and a little dazed.

Then he looks at Vernon again in that posture of rapt alertness.

"I got the hammer too," Vernon says. "Looks like we ought to done already got that chalk-line. It ought to floated."

"Floated clean away," Jewel says. "We wont get it. We ought to find the saw, though."

"I reckon so," Vernon says. He looks at the water. "That chalk-line, too. What else did he have?"

"He aint talked yet," Jewel says, entering the water. He looks back at me. "You go back and get him roused up to talk," he says.

"Pa's there," I say. I follow Jewel into the water, along the rope. It feels alive in my hand, bellied faintly in a prolonged and resonant arc. Vernon is watching me.

"You better go," he says. "You better be there."

"Let's see what else we can get before it washes on down," I say.

We hold to the rope, the current curling and dimpling about our shoulders. But beneath that false blandness the true force of it leans against us lazily. I had not thought that water in July could be so cold. It is like hands molding and prodding at the very bones. Vernon is still looking back toward the bank.

"Reckon it'll hold us all?" he says. We too look back, following the rigid bar of the rope as it rises from the water to the tree and Vardaman crouched a little beside it, watching us. "Wish my mule wouldn't strike out for home," Vernon says.

"Come on," Jewel says. "Let's get outen here."

We submerge in turn, holding to the rope, being clutched by one another while the cold wall of the water sucks the slanting mud backward and upstream from beneath our feet and we are suspended so, groping along the cold bottom. Even the mud there is not still. It has a chill, scouring quality, as though the earth under us were in motion too. We touch and fumble at one another's extended arms, letting ourselves go cautiously against the rope; or, erect in turn, watch the water suck and boil where one of the other two gropes beneath the surface. Pa has come down to the shore, watching us.

Vernon comes up, streaming, his face sloped down into his pursed blowing mouth. His mouth is bluish, like a circle of weathered rubber. He has the rule.

"He'll be glad of that," I say. "It's right new. He bought it just last month out of the catalogue."

"If we just knowed for sho what else," Vernon says, looking over his shoulder and then turning to face where Jewel had disappeared. "Didn't he go down fore me?" Vernon says.

"I dont know," I say. "I think so. Yes. Yes, he did."

We watch the thick curling surface, streaming away from us in slow whorls.

"Give him a pull on the rope," Vernon says.

"He's on your end of it," I say.

"Aint nobody on my end of it," he says.

"Pull it in," I say. But he has already done that, holding the end above the water; and then we see Jewel. He is ten yards away; he comes up, blowing, and looks at us, tossing his long hair back with a jerk of his head, then he looks toward the bank; we can see him filling his lungs.

"Jewel," Vernon says, not loud, but his voice going full and clear along the water, peremptory yet tactful. "It'll be back here. Better come back."

Jewel dives again. We stand there, leaning back against the current, watching the water where he disappeared, holding the dead rope between us like two men holding the nozzle of a fire hose, waiting for the water. Suddenly Dewey Dell is behind us in the water. "You make him come back," she says. "Jewel!" she says. He comes up again, tossing his hair back from his eyes. He is swimming now, toward the bank, the current sweeping him downstream quartering. "You, Jewel!" Dewey Dell says. We stand holding the rope and see him gain the bank and climb out. As he rises from the water, he stoops and picks up something. He comes back along the bank. He has found the chalkline. He comes opposite us and stands there, looking about as if he were seeking something. Pa goes on down the bank. He is going back to look at the mules again where their round bodies float and rub quietly together in the slack water within the bend.

"What did you do with the hammer, Vernon?" Jewel says.

"I give it to him," Vernon says, jerking his head at Vardaman. Vardaman is looking after pa. Then he looks at Jewel. "With the square." Vernon is watching Jewel. He moves toward the bank, passing Dewey Dell and me.

"You get on out of here," I say. She says nothing, looking at Jewel and Vernon.

"Where's the hammer?" Jewel says. Vardaman scuttles up the bank and fetches it.

"It's heavier than the saw," Vernon says. Jewel is tying the end of the chalk-line about the hammer shaft.

"Hammer's got the most wood in it," Jewel says. He and Vernon face one another, watching Jewel's hands.

"And flatter, too," Vernon says. "It'd float three to one, almost. Try the plane."

Jewel looks at Vernon. Vernon is tall, too; long and lean, eye to eye they stand in their close wet clothes. Lon Quick could look even at a cloudy sky and tell the time to ten minutes. Big Lon I mean, not little Lon.

"Why dont you get out of the water?" I say.

"It wont float like a saw," Jewel says.

"It'll float nigher to a saw than a hammer will," Vernon says.

"Bet you," Jewel says.

"I wont bet," Vernon says.

They stand there, watching Jewel's still hands.

"Hell," Jewel says. "Get the plane, then."

So they get the plane and tie it to the chalk-line and enter the water again. Pa comes back along the bank. He stops for a while and looks at us, hunched, mournful, like a failing steer or an old tall bird.

Vernon and Jewel return, leaning against the current. "Get out of the way," Jewel says to Dewey Dell. "Get out of the water."

She crowds against me a little so they can pass, Jewel holding the plane high as though it were perishable, the blue string trailing back over his shoulder. They pass us and stop; they fall to arguing quietly about just where the wagon went over.

"Darl ought to know," Vernon says. They look at me.

"I dont know," I says. "I wasn't there that long."

"Hell," Jewel says. They move on, gingerly, leaning against the current, reading the ford with their feet.

"Have you got a holt of the rope?" Vernon says. Jewel does not answer. He glances back at the shore, calculant, then at the water. He flings the plane outward, letting the string run through his fingers, his fingers turning blue where it runs over them. When the line stops, he hands it back to Vernon.

"Better let me go this time," Vernon says. Again Jewel does not answer; we watch him duck beneath the surface.

"Jewel," Dewey Dell whimpers.

"It aint so deep there," Vernon says. He does not look back. He is watching the water where Jewel went under.

When Jewel comes up he has the saw.

When we pass the wagon pa is standing beside it, scrubbing at the two mud smears with a handful of leaves. Against the jungle Jewel's horse looks like a patchwork quilt hung on a line.

Cash has not moved. We stand above him, holding the plane, the saw, the hammer, the square, the rule, the chalk-line, while Dewey Dell squats and lifts Cash's head. "Cash," she says; "Cash."

He opens his eyes, staring profoundly up at our inverted faces.

"If ever was such a misfortunate man," pa says.

"Look, Cash," we say, holding the tools up so he can see; "what else did you have?"

He tries to speak, rolling his head, shutting his eyes. "Cash," we say; "Cash."

It is to vomit he is turning his head. Dewey Dell wipes his mouth on the wet hem of her dress; then he can speak.

"It's his saw-set," Jewel says. "The new one he bought when he bought the rule." He moves, turning away. Vernon looks up after him, still squatting. Then he rises and follows Jewel down to the water.

"If ever was such a misfortunate man," pa says. He

looms tall above us as we squat; he looks like a figure carved clumsily from tough wood by a drunken caricaturist. "It's a trial," he says. "But I dont begrudge her it. No man can say I begrudge her it." Dewey Dell has laid Cash's head back on the folded coat, twisting his head a little to avoid the vomit. Beside him his tools lie. "A fellow might call it lucky it was the same leg he broke when he fell offen that church," pa says. "But I dont begrudge her it."

Jewel and Vernon are in the river again. From here they do not appear to violate the surface at all; it is as though it had severed them both at a single blow, the two torsos moving with infinitesimal and ludicrous care upon the surface. It looks peaceful, like machinery does after you have watched it and listened to it for a long time. As though the clotting which is you had dissolved into the myriad original motion, and seeing and hearing in themselves blind and deaf; fury in itself quiet with stagnation. Squatting, Dewey Dell's wet dress shapes for the dead eyes of three blind men those mammalian ludicrosities which are the horizons and the valleys of the earth.

Cash

It wasn't on a balance. I told them that if they wanted it to tote and ride on a balance, they would have to

Cora

One day we were talking. She had never been pure religious, not even after that summer at the camp meeting when Brother Whitfield wrestled with her spirit, singled her out and strove with the vanity in her mortal heart, and I said to her many a time, "God gave you children to comfort your hard human lot and for a token of His own suffering and love, for in love you conceived and bore them." I said that because she took God's love and her duty to Him too much as a matter of course, and such conduct is not pleasing to Him. I said, "He gave us the gift to raise our voices in His undying praise" because I said there is more rejoicing in heaven over one sinner than over a hundred that never sinned. And she said, "My daily life

is an acknowledgment and expiation of my sin" and
I said "Who are you, to say what is sin and what is
not sin? It is the Lord's part to judge; ours to praise
His mercy and His holy name in the hearing of our
fellow mortals" because He alone can see into the
heart, and just because a woman's life is right in the
sight of man, she cant know if there is no sin in her
heart without she opens her heart to the Lord and re-
ceives His grace. I said, "Just because you have been
a faithful wife is no sign that there is no sin in your
heart, and just because your life is hard is no sign that
the Lord's grace is absolving you." And she said, "I
know my own sin. I know that I deserve my punishment. I do not begrudge it." And I said, "It is out of
your vanity that you would judge sin and salvation in
the Lord's place. It is our mortal lot to suffer and to
raise our voices in praise of Him who judges the sin
and offers the salvation through our trials and tribula-
tions time out of mind amen. Not even after Brother
Whitfield, a godly man if ever one breathed God's
breath, prayed for you and strove as never a man
could except him," I said.

Because it is not us that can judge our sins or know
what is sin in the Lord's eyes. She has had a hard life,
but so does every woman. But you'd think from the
way she talked that she knew more about sin and salvation than the Lord God Himself, than them who
have strove and labored with the sin in this human
world. When the only sin she ever committed was being partial to Jewel that never loved her and was
its own punishment, in preference to Darl that was
touched by God Himself and considered queer by us
mortals and that did love her. I said, "There is your
sin. And your punishment too. Jewel is your punish-

ment. But where is your salvation? And life is short
enough," I said, "to win eternal grace in. And God is
a jealous God. It is His to judge and to mete; not
yours."

"I know," she said. "I—" Then she stopped, and I
said,

"Know what?"

"Nothing," she said. "He is my cross and he will be
my salvation. He will save me from the water and
from the fire. Even though I have laid down my life,
he will save me."

"How do you know, without you open your heart to
Him and lift your voice in His praise?" I said. Then
I realised that she did not mean God. I realised that
out of the vanity of her heart she had spoken sacrilege. And I went down on my knees right there. I
begged her to kneel and open her heart and cast from
it the devil of vanity and cast herself upon the mercy
of the Lord. But she wouldn't. She just sat there, lost
in her vanity and her pride, that had closed her heart
to God and set that selfish mortal boy in His place.
Kneeling there I prayed for her. I prayed for that poor
blind woman as I had never prayed for me and mine.

Addie

---

she's a teacher

In the afternoon when school was out and the last one had left with his little dirty snuffling nose, instead of going home I would go down the hill to the spring where I could be quiet and hate them. It would be quiet there then, with the water bubbling up and away and the sun slanting quiet in the trees and the quiet smelling of damp and rotting leaves and new earth; especially in the early spring, for it was worst then.

I could just remember how my father used to say that the reason for living was to get ready to stay dead a long time. And when I would have to look at them day after day, each with his and her secret and selfish thought, and blood strange to each other blood and

wants to know what's going on

strange to mine, and think that this seemed to be the
only way I could get ready to stay dead, I would hate
my father for having ever planted me. I would look
forward to the times when they faulted, so I could
whip them. When the switch fell I could feel it upon
my flesh; when it welted and ridged it was my blood
that ran, and I would think with each blow of the
switch: Now you are aware of me! Now I am something in your secret and selfish life, who have marked
your blood with my own for ever and ever.

And so I took Anse. I saw him pass the school house
three or four times before I learned that he was driving four miles out of his way to do it. I noticed then
how he was beginning to hump—a tall man and young
—so that he looked already like a tall bird hunched
in the cold weather, on the wagon seat. He would pass
the school house, the wagon creaking slow, his head
turning slow to watch the door of the school house as
the wagon passed, until he went on around the curve
and out of sight. One day I went to the door and stood
there when he passed. When he saw me he looked
quickly away and did not look back again.

In the early spring it was worst. Sometimes I thought
that I could not bear it, lying in bed at night, with
the wild geese going north and their honking coming
faint and high and wild out of the wild darkness, and
during the day it would seem as though I couldn't
wait for the last one to go so I could go down to the
spring. And so when I looked up that day and saw
Anse standing there in his Sunday clothes, turning his
hat round and round in his hands, I said:

"If you've got any womenfolks, why in the world
dont they make you get your hair cut?"

"I aint got none," he said. Then he said suddenly,

driving his eyes at me like two hounds in a strange yard: "That's what I come to see you about."

"And make you hold your shoulders up," I said. "You haven't got any? But you've got a house. They tell me you've got a house and a good farm. And you live there alone, doing for yourself, do you?" He just looked at me, turning the hat in his hands. "A new house," I said. "Are you going to get married?"

And he said again, holding his eyes to mine: "That's what I come to see you about."

Later he told me, "I aint got no people. So that wont be no worry to you. I dont reckon you can say the same."

"No. I have people. In Jefferson."

His face fell a little. "Well, I got a little property. I'm forehanded; I got a good honest name. I know how town folks are, but maybe when they talk to me . . ."

"They might listen," I said. "But they'll be hard to talk to." He was watching my face. "They're in the cemetery."

"But your living kin," he said. "They'll be different."

"Will they?" I said. "I dont know. I never had any other kind."

So I took Anse. And when I knew that I had Cash, I knew that living was terrible and that this was the answer to it. That was when I learned that words are no good; that words dont ever fit even what they are trying to say at. When he was born I knew that motherhood was invented by someone who had to have a word for it because the ones that had the children didn't care whether there was a word for it or not. I knew that fear was invented by someone that had never had the fear; pride, who never had the pride. I knew that it had been, not that they had dirty noses, but that we had had to use one another by words like spiders dangling by their mouths from a beam, swinging and twisting and never touching, and that only through the blows of the switch could my blood and their blood flow as one stream. I knew that it had been, not that my aloneness had to be violated over and over each day, but that it had never been violated until Cash came. Not even by Anse in the nights.

He had a word, too. Love, he called it. But I had been used to words for a long time. I knew that that word was like the others: just a shape to fill a lack; that when the right time came, you wouldn't need a word for that anymore than for pride or fear. Cash did not need to say it to me nor I to him, and I would say, Let Anse use it, if he wants to. So that it was Anse or love; love or Anse: it didn't matter.

I would think that even while I lay with him in the dark and Cash asleep in the cradle within the swing of my hand. I would think that if he were to wake and cry, I would suckle him, too. Anse or love: it didn't matter. My aloneness had been violated and then made whole again by the violation: time, Anse, love, what you will, outside the circle.

Then I found that I had Darl. At first I would not believe it. Then I believed that I would kill Anse. It was as though he had tricked me, hidden within a word like within a paper screen and struck me in the back through it. But then I realised that I had been tricked by words older than Anse or love, and that the same word had tricked Anse too, and that my revenge would be that he would never know I was taking revenge. And when Darl was born I asked Anse to promise to take me back to Jefferson when I died, because I knew that father had been right, even when he couldn't have known he was right anymore than I could have known I was wrong.

"Nonsense," Anse said; "you and me aint nigh done chapping yet, with just two."

He did not know that he was dead, then. Sometimes I would lie by him in the dark, hearing the land that was now of my blood and flesh, and I would think: Anse. Why Anse. Why are you Anse. I would think about his name until after a while I could see the word as a shape, a vessel, and I would watch him liquefy and flow into it like cold molasses flowing out of the darkness into the vessel, until the jar stood full and motionless: a significant shape profoundly without life like an empty door frame; and then I would find that I had forgotten the name of the jar. I would think: The shape of my body where I used to be a virgin is in the shape of a   and I couldn't think *Anse*, couldn't remember *Anse*. It was not that I could think of myself as no longer unvirgin, because I was three now. And when I would think *Cash* and *Darl* that way until their names would die and solidify into a shape and then fade away, I would say, All right. It doesn't matter. It doesn't matter what they call them.

And so when Cora Tull would tell me I was not a true mother, I would think how words go straight up in a thin line, quick and harmless, and how terribly doing goes along the earth, clinging to it, so that after a while the two lines are too far apart for the same person to straddle from one to the other; and that sin and love and fear are just sounds that people who never sinned nor loved nor feared have for what they

never had and cannot have until they forget the words.
Like Cora, who could never even cook.

She would tell me what I owed to my children and
to Anse and to God. I gave Anse the children. I did
not ask for them. I did not even ask him for what he
could have given me: not-Anse. That was my duty to
him, to not ask that, and that duty I fulfilled. I would
be I; I would let him be the shape and echo of his
word. That was more than he asked, because he could
not have asked for that and been Anse, using himself
so with a word.

Anse: And then he died. He did not know he was dead. I
would lie by him in the dark, hearing the dark land
talking of God's love and His beauty and His sin;
hearing the dark voicelessness in which the words are
the deeds, and the other words that are not deeds, that
are just the gaps in peoples' lacks, coming down like
the cries of the geese out of the wild darkness in the
old terrible nights, fumbling at the deeds like orphans
to whom are pointed out in a crowd two faces and
told, That is your father, your mother.

I believed that I had found it. I believed that the
reason was the duty to the alive, to the terrible blood,
the red bitter flood boiling through the land. I would
think of sin as I would think of the clothes we both
wore in the world's face, of the circumspection necessary because he was he and I was I; the sin the more
utter and terrible since he was the instrument or-
dained by God who created the sin, to sanctify that
sin He had created. While I waited for him in the
woods, waiting for him before he saw me, I would
think of him as dressed in sin. I would think of him
as thinking of me as dressed also in sin, he the more
beautiful since the garment which he had exchanged

Sinning w/Whitfield

for sin was sanctified. I would think of the sin as garments which we would remove in order to shape and coerce the terrible blood to the forlorn echo of the dead word high in the air. Then I would lay with Anse again—I did not lie to him: I just refused, just as I refused my breast to Cash and Darl after their time was up—hearing the dark land talking the voiceless speech.   B

I hid nothing. I tried to deceive no one. I would not have cared. I merely took the precautions that he thought necessary for his sake, not for my safety, but just as I wore clothes in the world's face. And I would think then when Cora talked to me, of how the high dead words in time seemed to lose even the significance of their dead sound.

Then it was over. Over in the sense that he was gone and I knew that, see him again though I would, I would never again see him coming swift and secret to me in the woods dressed in sin like a gallant garment already blowing aside with the speed of his secret coming.

But for me it was not over. I mean, over in the sense of beginning and ending, because to me there was no beginning nor ending to anything then. I even held Anse refraining still, not that I was holding him recessional, but as though nothing else had ever been. My children were of me alone, of the wild blood boiling along the earth, of me and of all that lived; of none and of all. Then I found that I had Jewel. When I waked to remember to discover it, he was two months gone.

My father said that the reason for living is getting ready to stay dead. I knew at last what he meant and that he could not have known what he meant himself,

because a man cannot know anything about cleaning
up the house afterward. And so I have cleaned my
house. With Jewel—I lay by the lamp, holding up my
own head, watching him cap and suture it before he
breathed—the wild blood boiled away and the sound
of it ceased. Then there was only the milk, warm and
calm, and I lying calm in the slow silence, getting
ready to clean my house.

I gave Anse Dewey Dell to negative Jewel. Then I
gave him Vardaman to replace the child I had robbed
him of. And now he has three children that are his
and not mine. And then I could get ready to die.

One day I was talking to Cora. She prayed for me
because she believed I was blind to sin, wanting me
to kneel and pray too, because people to whom sin is
just a matter of words, to them salvation is just words
too.

Whitfield

When they told me she was dying, all that night I wrestled with Satan, and I emerged victorious. I woke to the enormity of my sin; I saw the true light at last, and I fell on my knees and confessed to God and asked His guidance and received it. "Rise," He said; "repair to that home in which you have put a living lie, among those people with whom you have outraged My Word; confess your sin aloud. It is for them, for that deceived husband, to forgive you: not I."

So I went. I heard that Tull's bridge was gone; I said "Thanks, O Lord, O Mighty Ruler of all"; for by those dangers and difficulties which I should have to surmount I saw that He had not abandoned me; that my reception again into His holy peace and love

would be the sweeter for it. "Just let me not perish before I have begged the forgiveness of the man whom
I betrayed," I prayed; "let me not be too late; let
not the tale of mine and her transgression come from
her lips instead of mine. She had sworn then that she
would never tell it, but eternity is a fearsome thing to
face: have I not wrestled thigh to thigh with Satan
myself? let me not have also the sin of her broken
vow upon my soul. Let not the waters of Thy Mighty
Wrath encompass me until I have cleansed my soul in
the presence of them whom I injured."

It was His hand that bore me safely above the
flood, that fended from me the dangers of the waters.
My horse was frightened, and my own heart failed me
as the logs and the uprooted trees bore down upon
my littleness. But not my soul: time after time I saw
them averted at destruction's final instant, and I lifted
my voice above the noise of the flood: "Praise to Thee,
O Mighty Lord and King. By this token shall I cleanse
my soul and gain again into the fold of Thy undying
love."

I knew then that forgiveness was mine. The flood,
the danger, behind, and as I rode on across the firm
earth again and the scene of my Gethsemane drew
closer and closer, I framed the words which I should
use. I would enter the house; I would stop her before
she had spoken; I would say to her husband: "Anse,
I have sinned. Do with me as you will."

It was already as though it were done. My soul felt
freer, quieter than it had in years; already I seemed
to dwell in abiding peace again as I rode on. To either
side I saw His hand; in my heart I could hear His
voice: "Courage. I am with thee."

Then I reached Tull's house. His youngest girl came

out and called to me as I was passing. She told me that she was already dead.

I have sinned, O Lord. Thou knowest the extent of my remorse and the will of my spirit. But He is merciful; He will accept the will for the deed, Who knew that when I framed the words of my confession it was to Anse I spoke them, even though he was not there. It was He in His infinite wisdom that restrained the tale from her dying lips as she lay surrounded by those who loved and trusted her; mine the travail by water which I sustained by the strength of His hand. Praise to Thee in Thy bounteous and omnipotent love; O praise.

I entered the house of bereavement, the lowly dwelling where another erring mortal lay while her soul faced the awful and irrevocable judgment, peace to her ashes.

"God's grace upon this house," I said.

Darl

On the horse he rode up to Armstid's and *came back on the horse,* leading Armstid's team. We hitched up and laid Cash on top of Addie. When we laid him down he vomited again, but he got his head over the wagon bed in time.

"He taken a lick in the stomach, too," Vernon said.

"The horse may have kicked him in the stomach too," I said. "Did he kick you in the stomach, Cash?"

He tried to say something. Dewey Dell wiped his mouth again.

"What's he say?" Vernon said.

"What is it, Cash?" Dewey Dell said. She leaned down. "His tools," she said. Vernon got them and put them into the wagon. Dewey Dell lifted Cash's head so he could see. We drove on, Dewey Dell and I sitting beside Cash to steady him *and he riding on ahead on the horse.* Vernon stood watching us for a while. Then he turned and went back toward the bridge. He walked gingerly, beginning to flap the wet sleeves of his shirt as though he had just got wet.

He was sitting the horse before the gate. Armstid was waiting at the gate. We stopped *and he got down* and we lifted Cash down and carried him into the house, where Mrs Armstid had the bed ready. We left her and Dewey Dell undressing him.

We followed pa out to the wagon. He went back and got into the wagon and drove on, we following on foot, into the lot. The wetting had helped, because Armstid said, "You're welcome to the house. You can put it there." *He followed, leading the horse, and stood beside the wagon, the reins in his hand.*

"I thank you," pa said. "We'll use in the shed yonder. I know it's a imposition on you."

"You're welcome to the house," Armstid said. *He had that wooden look on his face again; that bold, surly, high-colored rigid look like his face and eyes were two colors of wood, the wrong one pale and the wrong one dark. His shirt was beginning to dry, but it still clung close upon him when he moved.*

"She would appreciate it," pa said.

We took the team out and rolled the wagon back under the shed. One side of the shed was open.

"It wont rain under," Armstid said. "But if you'd rather . . ."

Back of the barn was some rusted sheets of tin roofing. We took two of them and propped them against the open side.

"You're welcome to the house," Armstid said.

"I thank you," pa said. "I'd take it right kind if you'd give them a little snack."

"Sho," Armstid said. "Lula'll have supper ready soon as she gets Cash comfortable." *He had gone back to the horse and he was taking the saddle off, his damp shirt lapping flat to him when he moved.*

Pa wouldn't come in the house.

"Come in and eat," Armstid said. "It's nigh ready."

"I wouldn't crave nothing," pa said. "I thank you."

"You come in and dry and eat," Armstid said. "It'll be all right here."

"It's for her," pa said. "It's for her sake I am taking the food. I got no team, no nothing. But she will be grateful to ere a one of you."

"Sho," Armstid said. "You folks come in and dry."

But after Armstid gave pa a drink, he felt better, and when we went in to see about Cash *he hadn't come in with us. When I looked back he was leading the horse into the barn* he was already talking about getting another team, and by supper time he had good as bought it. *He is down there in the barn, sliding fluidly past the gaudy lunging swirl, into the stall with it. He climbs onto the manger and drags the hay down and leaves the stall and seeks and finds the curry-comb. Then he returns and slips quickly past the single crashing thump and up against the horse, where it cannot overreach. He applies the curry-comb, holding himself within the horse's striking radius with the agility of an acrobat, cursing the horse in a whisper of obscene caress. Its head flashes back, tooth-cropped; its eyes roll in the dusk like marbles on a gaudy velvet cloth as he strikes it upon the face with the back of the curry-comb.*

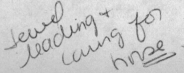
Jewel leading + caring for horse.

Armstid

But time I give him another sup of whisky and supper was about ready, he had done already bought a team from somebody, on a credit. Picking and choosing he were by then, saying how he didn't like this span and wouldn't put his money in nothing so-and-so owned, not even a hen coop.

"You might try Snopes," I said. "He's got three-four span. Maybe one of them would suit you."

Then he begun to mumble his mouth, looking at me like it was me that owned the only span of mules in the county and wouldn't sell them to him, when I knew that like as not it would be my team that would ever get them out of the lot at all. Only I dont know what they would do with them, if they had a team.

Littlejohn had told me that the levee through Haley bottom had done gone for two miles and that the only way to get to Jefferson would be to go around by Mottson. But that was Anse's business.

"He's a close man to trade with," he says, mumbling his mouth. But when I give him another sup after supper, he cheered up some. He was aiming to go back to the barn and set up with her. Maybe he thought that if he just stayed down there ready to take out, Santa Claus would maybe bring him a span of mules. "But I reckon I can talk him around," he says. "A man'll always help a fellow in a tight, if he's got ere a drop of Christian blood in him."

"Of course you're welcome to the use of mine," I said, me knowing how much he believed that was the reason.

"I thank you," he said. "She'll want to go in ourn," and him knowing how much I believed that was the reason.

After supper Jewel rode over to the Bend to get Peabody. I heard he was to be there today at Varner's. Jewel come back about midnight. Peabody had gone down below Inverness somewhere, but Uncle Billy come back with him, with his satchel of horse-physic. Like he says, a man aint so different from a horse or a mule, come long come short, except a mule or a horse has got a little more sense. "What you been into now, boy?" he says, looking at Cash. "Get me a mattress and a chair and a glass of whisky," he says.

He made Cash drink the whisky, then he run Anse out of the room. "Lucky it was the same leg he broke last summer," Anse says, mournful, mumbling and blinking. "That's something."

We folded the mattress across Cash's legs and set

the chair on the mattress and me and Jewel set on the chair and the gal held the lamp and Uncle Billy taken a chew of tobacco and went to work. Cash fought pretty hard for a while, until he fainted. Then he laid still, with big balls of sweat standing on his face like they had started to roll down and then stopped to wait for him.

When he waked up, Uncle Billy had done packed up and left. He kept on trying to say something until the gal leaned down and wiped his mouth. "It's his tools," she said.

"I brought them in," Darl said. "I got them."

He tried to talk again; she leaned down. "He wants to see them," she said. So Darl brought them in where he could see them. They shoved them under the side of the bed, where he could reach his hand and touch them when he felt better. Next morning Anse taken that horse and rode over to the Bend to see Snopes. Him and Jewel stood in the lot talking a while, then Anse got on the horse and rode off. I reckon that was the first time Jewel ever let anybody ride that horse, and until Anse come back he hung around in that swole-up way, watching the road like he was half a mind to take out after Anse and get the horse back.

Along toward nine oclock it begun to get hot. That was when I see the first buzzard. Because of the wetting, I reckon. Anyway it wasn't until well into the day that I see them. Lucky the breeze was setting away from the house, so it wasn't until well into the morning. But soon as I see them it was like I could smell it in the field a mile away from just watching them, and them circling and circling for everybody in the county to see what was in my barn.

I was still a good half a mile from the house when

I heard that boy yelling. I thought maybe he might have fell into the well or something, so I whipped up and come into the lot on the lope.

buzzard There must have been a dozen of them setting along the ridge-pole of the barn, and that boy was chasing another one around the lot like it was a turkey and it just lifting enough to dodge him and go flopping back to the roof of the shed again where he had found it setting on the coffin. It had got hot then, right, and the breeze had dropped or changed or something, so I went and found Jewel, but Lula come out.

"You got to do something," she said. "It's a outrage."

"That's what I aim to do," I said.

"It's a outrage," she said. "He should be lawed for treating her so."

"He's getting her into the ground the best he can," I said. So I found Jewel and asked him if he didn't want to take one of the mules and go over to the Bend and see about Anse. He didn't say nothing. He just looked at me with his jaws going bone-white and them bone-white eyes of hisn, then he went and begun to call Darl.

"What you fixing to do?" I said.

He didn't answer. Darl come out. "Come on," Jewel said.

"What you aim to do?" Darl said.

"Going to move the wagon," Jewel said over his shoulder.

"Dont be a fool," I said. "I never meant nothing. You couldn't help it." And Darl hung back too, but nothing wouldn't suit Jewel.

"Shut your goddamn mouth," he says.

"It's got to be somewhere," Darl said. "We'll take out soon as pa gets back."

"You wont help me?" Jewel says, them white eyes of hisn kind of blaring and his face shaking like he had a aguer.

"No," Darl said. "I wont. Wait till pa gets back."

So I stood in the door and watched him push and haul at that wagon. It was on a downhill, and once I thought he was fixing to beat out the back end of the shed. Then the dinner bell rung. I called him, but he didn't look around. "Come on to dinner," I said. "Tell that boy." But he didn't answer, so I went on to dinner. The gal went down to get that boy, but she come back without him. About half through dinner we heard him yelling again, running that buzzard out.

"It's a outrage," Lula said; "a outrage."

"He's doing the best he can," I said. "A fellow dont trade with Snopes in thirty minutes. They'll set in the shade all afternoon to dicker."

"Do?" she says. "Do? He's done too much, already."

And I reckon he had. Trouble is, his quitting was just about to start our doing. He couldn't buy no team from nobody, let alone Snopes, withouten he had something to mortgage he didn't know would mortgage yet. And so when I went back to the field I looked at my mules and same as told them goodbye for a spell. And when I come back that evening and the sun shining all day on that shed, I wasn't so sho I would regret it.

He come riding up just as I went out to the porch, where they all was. He looked kind of funny: kind of more hang-dog than common, and kind of proud too. Like he had done something he thought was cute but wasn't so sho now how other folks would take it.

"I got a team," he said.

"You bought a team from Snopes?" I said.

"I reckon Snopes aint the only man in this country that can drive a trade," he said.

"Sho," I said. He was looking at Jewel, with that funny look, but Jewel had done got down from the porch and was going toward the horse. To see what Anse had done to it, I reckon.

"Jewel," Anse says. Jewel looked back. "Come here," Anse says. Jewel come back a little and stopped again. "What you want?" he said.

"So you got a team from Snopes," I said. "He'll send them over tonight, I reckon? You'll want a early start tomorrow, long as you'll have to go by Mottson."

Then he quit looking like he had been for a while. He got that badgered look like he used to have, mumbling his mouth.

"I do the best I can," he said. "Fore God, if there were ere a man in the living world suffered the trials and floutings I have suffered."

"A fellow that just beat Snopes in a trade ought to feel pretty good," I said. "What did you give him, Anse?"

He didn't look at me. "I give a chattel mortgage on my cultivator and seeder," he said.

"But they aint worth forty dollars. How far do you aim to get with a forty dollar team?"

They were all watching him now, quiet and steady. Jewel was stopped, halfway back, waiting to go on to the horse. "I give other things," Anse said. He begun to mumble his mouth again, standing there like he was waiting for somebody to hit him and him with his mind already made up not to do nothing about it.

"What other things?" Darl said.

"Hell," I said. "You take my team. You can bring them back. I'll get along someway."

"So that's what you were doing in Cash's clothes last night," Darl said. He said it just like he was reading it outen the paper. Like he never give a durn himself one way or the other. Jewel had come back now, standing there, looking at Anse with them marble eyes of hisn. "Cash aimed to buy that talking machine from Suratt with that money," Darl said.

Anse stood there, mumbling his mouth. Jewel watched him. He aint never blinked yet.

"But that's just eight dollars more," Darl said, in that voice like he was just listening and never give a durn himself. "That still wont buy a team."

Anse looked at Jewel, quick, kind of sliding his eyes that way, then he looked down again. "God knows, if there were ere a man," he says. Still they didn't say nothing. They just watched him, waiting, and him sliding his eyes toward their feet and up their legs but no higher. "And the horse," he says.

"What horse?" Jewel said. Anse just stood there. I be durn, if a man cant keep the upper hand of his sons, he ought to run them away from home, no matter how big they are. And if he cant do that, I be durn if he oughtn't to leave himself. I be durn if I wouldn't. "You mean, you tried to swap my horse?" Jewel says.

Anse stands there, dangle-armed. "For fifteen years I aint had a tooth in my head," he says. "God knows it. He knows in fifteen years I aint et the victuals He aimed for man to eat to keep his strength up, and me saving a nickel here and a nickel there so my family wouldn't suffer it, to buy them teeth so I could eat God's appointed food. I give that money. I thought that if I could do without eating, my sons could do without riding. God knows I did."

Jewel stands with his hands on his hips, looking at Anse. Then he looks away. He looked out across the field, his face still as a rock, like it was somebody else talking about somebody else's horse and him not even listening. Then he spit, slow, and said "Hell" and he turned and went on to the gate and unhitched the horse and got on it. It was moving when he come into the saddle and by the time he was on it they was tearing down the road like the Law might have been behind them. They went out of sight that way, the two of them looking like some kind of a spotted cyclone.

"Well," I says. "You take my team," I said. But he wouldn't do it. And they wouldn't even stay, and that boy chasing them buzzards all day in the hot sun until he was nigh as crazy as the rest of them. "Leave Cash here, anyway," I said. But they wouldn't do that. They made a pallet for him with quilts on top of the coffin and laid him on it and set his tools by him, and we put my team in and hauled the wagon about a mile down the road.

"If we'll bother you here," Anse says, "just say so."

"Sho," I said. "It'll be fine here. Safe, too. Now let's go back and eat supper."

"I thank you," Anse said. "We got a little something in the basket. We can make out."

"Where'd you get it?" I said.

"We brought it from home."

"But it'll be stale now," I said. "Come and get some hot victuals."

But they wouldn't come. "I reckon we can make

out," Anse said. So I went home and et and taken a basket back to them and tried again to make them come back to the house.

"I thank you," he said. "I reckon we can make out." So I left them there, squatting around a little fire, waiting; God knows what for.

I come on home. I kept thinking about them there, and about that fellow tearing away on that horse. And that would be the last they would see of him. And I be durn if I could blame him. Not for wanting to not give up his horse, but for getting shut of such a durn fool as Anse.

Or that's what I thought then. Because be durn if there aint something about a durn fellow like Anse that seems to make a man have to help him, even ✗ when he knows he'll be wanting to kick himself next minute. Because about a hour after breakfast next morning Eustace Grimm that works Snopes' place come up with a span of mules, hunting Anse.

"I thought him and Anse never traded," I said.

"Sho," Eustace said. "All they liked was the horse. Like I said to Mr Snopes, he was letting this team go for fifty dollars, because if his uncle Flem had a just kept them Texas horses when he owned them, Anse wouldn't a never—"

"The horse?" I said. "Anse's boy taken that horse and cleared out last night, probably halfway to Texas by now, and Anse—"

"I didn't know who brung it," Eustace said. "I never see them. I just found the horse in the barn this morning when I went to feed, and I told Mr Snopes and he said to bring the team on over here."

Well, that'll be the last they'll ever see of him now, sho enough. Come Christmas time they'll maybe get a postal card from him in Texas, I reckon. And if it hadn't a been Jewel, I reckon it'd a been me; I owe him that much, myself. I be durn if Anse dont conjure a man, some way. I be durn if he aint a sight.

Vardaman

Now there are seven of them, in little tall black circles.

"Look, Darl," I say; "see?"

He looks up. We watch them in little tall black circles of not-moving.

"Yesterday there were just four," I say.

There were more than four on the barn.

"Do you know what I would do if he tries to light on the wagon again?" I say.

"What would you do?" Darl says.

"I wouldn't let him light on her," I say. "I wouldn't let him light on Cash, either."

Cash is sick. He is sick on the box. But my mother is a fish.

"We got to get some medicine in Mottson," pa says. "I reckon we'll just have to."

"How do you feel, Cash?" Darl says.

"It dont bother none," Cash says.

"Do you want it propped a little higher?" Darl says.

Cash has a broken leg. He has had two broken legs. He lies on the box with a quilt rolled under his head and a piece of wood under his knee.

"I reckon we ought to left him at Armstid's," pa says.

I haven't got a broken leg and pa hasn't and Darl hasn't and   "It's just the bumps," Cash says. "It kind of grinds together a little on a bump. It dont bother none." *Jewel has gone away. He and his horse went away one supper time*

"It's because she wouldn't have us beholden," pa says. "Fore God, I do the best that ere a man" *Is it because Jewel's mother is a horse Darl? I said.*

"Maybe I can draw the ropes a little tighter," Darl says. *That's why Jewel and I were both in the shed and she was in the wagon because the horse lives in the barn and I had to keep on running the buzzard away from*

"If you just would," Cash says. And Dewey Dell hasn't got a broken leg and I haven't. Cash is my brother.

We stop. When Darl loosens the rope Cash begins to sweat again. His teeth look out.

"Hurt?" Darl says.

"I reckon you better put it back," Cash says.

Darl puts the rope back, pulling hard. Cash's teeth look out.

"Hurt?" Darl says.

"It dont bother none," Cash says.

"Do you want pa to drive slower?" Darl says.

"No," Cash says. "Aint no time to hang back. It dont bother none."

"We'll have to get some medicine at Mottson," pa says. "I reckon we'll have to."

"Tell him to go on," Cash says. We go on. Dewey Dell leans back and wipes Cash's face. Cash is my brother. *But Jewel's mother is a horse. My mother is a fish. Darl says that when we come to the water again I might see her and Dewey Dell said, She's in the box; how could she have got out? She got out through the holes I bored, into the water I said, and when we come to the water again I am going to see her. My mother is not in the box. My mother does not smell like that. My mother is a fish*

"Those cakes will be in fine shape by the time we get to Jefferson," Darl says.

Dewey Dell does not look around.

"You better try to sell them in Mottson," Darl says.

"When will we get to Mottson, Darl?" I say.

"Tomorrow," Darl says. "If this team dont rack to pieces. Snopes must have fed them on sawdust."

"Why did he feed them on sawdust, Darl?" I say.

"Look," Darl says. "See?"

Now there are nine of them, tall in little black circles.

When we come to the foot of the hill pa stops and Darl and Dewey Dell and I get out. Cash cant walk because he has a broken leg. "Come up, mules," pa says. The mules walk hard; the wagon creaks. Darl and Dewey Dell and I walk behind the wagon, up the hill. When we come to the top of the hill pa stops and we get back into the wagon.

Now there are ten of them, tall in little tall black circles on the sky.

Moseley

I happened to look up, and saw her outside the window, looking in. Not close to the glass, and not looking at anything in particular; just standing there with her head turned this way and her eyes full on me and kind of blank too, like she was waiting for a sign. When I looked up again she was moving toward the door.

She kind of bumbled at the screen door a minute, like they do, and came in. She had on a stiff-brimmed straw hat setting on the top of her head and she was carrying a package wrapped in newspaper: I thought that she had a quarter or a dollar at the most, and that after she stood around a while she would maybe buy a cheap comb or a bottle of nigger toilet water, so I never disturbed her for a minute or so except to notice that she was pretty in a kind of sullen, awkward way, and that she looked a sight better in her gingham dress and her own complexion than she would after she bought whatever she would finally decide on. Or tell that she wanted. I knew that she had already decided before she came in. But you have to let them take their time. So I went on with what I was doing, figuring to let Albert wait on her when he caught up at the fountain, when he came back to me.

"That woman," he said. "You better see what she wants."

"What does she want?" I said.

"I dont know. I cant get anything out of her. You better wait on her."

So I went around the counter. I saw that she was barefooted, standing with her feet flat and easy on the floor, like she was used to it. She was looking at me, hard, holding the package; I saw she had about as black a pair of eyes as ever I saw, and she was a stranger. I never remembered seeing her in Mottson before. "What can I do for you?" I said.

Still she didn't say anything. She stared at me without winking. Then she looked back at the folks at the fountain. Then she looked past me, toward the back of the store.

"Do you want to look at some toilet things?" I said. "Or is it medicine you want?"

"That's it," she said. She looked quick back at the fountain again. So I thought maybe her ma or somebody had sent her in for some of this female dope and she was ashamed to ask for it. I knew she couldn't have a complexion like hers and use it herself, let alone not

being much more than old enough to barely know
what it was for. It's a shame, the way they poison
themselves with it. But a man's got to stock it or go
out of business in this country.

"Oh," I said. "What do you use? We have—" She
looked at me again, almost like she had said hush,
and looked toward the back of the store again.

"I'd liefer go back there," she said.

"All right," I said. You have to humor them. You
save time by it. I followed her to the back. She put
her hand on the gate. "There's nothing back there but
the prescription case," I said. "What do you want?"
She stopped and looked at me. It was like she had
taken some kind of a lid off her face, her eyes. It was
her eyes: kind of dumb and hopeful and sullenly willing to be disappointed all at the same time. But she
was in trouble of some sort; I could see that. "What's
your trouble?" I said. "Tell me what it is you want.
I'm pretty busy." I wasn't meaning to hurry her, but
a man just hasn't got the time they have out there.

"It's the female trouble," she said.

"Oh," I said. "Is that all?" I thought maybe she
was younger than she looked, and her first one had
scared her, or maybe one had been a little abnormal
as it will in young women. "Where's your ma?" I said.
"Haven't you got one?"

"She's out yonder in the wagon," she said.

"Why not talk to her about it before you take any
medicine," I said. "Any woman would have told you
about it." She looked at me, and I looked at her again
and said, "How old are you?"

"Seventeen," she said.

"Oh," I said. "I thought maybe you were . . ." She
was watching me. But then, in the eyes all of them

look like they had no age and knew everything in the world, anyhow. "Are you too regular, or not regular enough?"

She quit looking at me but she didn't move. "Yes," she said. "I reckon so. Yes."

"Well, which?" I said. "Dont you know?" It's a crime and a shame; but after all, they'll buy it from somebody. She stood there, not looking at me. "You want something to stop it?" I said. "Is that it?"

"No," she said. "That's it. It's already stopped."

"Well, what—" Her face was lowered a little, still, like they do in all their dealings with a man so he dont ever know just where the lightning will strike next. "You are not married, are you?" I said.

"No."

"Oh," I said. "And how long has it been since it stopped? about five months maybe?"

"It aint been but two," she said.

"Well, I haven't got anything in my store you want to buy," I said, "unless it's a nipple. And I'd advise you to buy that and go back home and tell your pa, if you have one, and let him make somebody buy you a wedding license. Was that all you wanted?"

But she just stood there, not looking at me.

"I got the money to pay you," she said.

"Is it your own, or did he act enough of a man to give you the money?"

"He give it to me. Ten dollars. He said that would be enough."

"A thousand dollars wouldn't be enough in my store and ten cents wouldn't be enough," I said. "You take my advice and go home and tell your pa or your brothers if you have any or the first man you come to in the road."

But she didn't move. "Lafe said I could get it at
the drugstore. He said to tell you me and him wouldn't
never tell nobody you sold it to us."

"And I just wish your precious Lafe had come for
it himself; that's what I wish. I dont know: I'd have
had a little respect for him then. And you can go back
and tell him I said so—if he aint halfway to Texas by
now, which I dont doubt. Me, a respectable druggist,
that's kept store and raised a family and been a
church-member for fifty-six years in this town. I'm
a good mind to tell your folks myself, if I can just
find who they are."

She looked at me now, her eyes and face kind of
blank again like when I first saw her through the
window. "I didn't know," she said. "He told me I
could get something at the drugstore. He said they
might not want to sell it to me, but if I had ten dollars
and told them I wouldn't never tell nobody . . ."

"He never said this drugstore," I said. "If he did
or mentioned my name, I defy him to prove it. I defy
him to repeat it or I'll prosecute him to the full extent
of the law, and you can tell him so."

"But maybe another drugstore would," she said.

"Then I dont want to know it. Me, that's—" Then
I looked at her. But it's a hard life they have; sometimes a man . . . if there can ever be any excuse for
sin, which it cant be. And then, life wasn't made to be
easy on folks: they wouldn't ever have any reason to
be good and die. "Look here," I said. "You get that
notion out of your head. The Lord gave you what you
have, even if He did use the devil to do it; you let
Him take it away from you if it's His will to do so.
You go on back to Lafe and you and him take that
ten dollars and get married with it."

"Lafe said I could get something at the drugstore," she said.

"Then go and get it," I said. "You wont get it here."

She went out, carrying the package, her feet making a little hissing on the floor. She bumbled again at the door and went out. I could see her through the glass going on down the street.

It was Albert told me about the rest of it. He said the wagon was stopped in front of Grummet's hardware store, with the ladies all scattering up and down the street with handkerchiefs to their noses, and a crowd of hard-nosed men and boys standing around the wagon, listening to the marshal arguing with the man. He was a kind of tall, gaunted man sitting on the wagon, saying it was a public street and he reckoned he had as much right there as anybody, and the marshal telling him he would have to move on; folks couldn't stand it. It had been dead eight days, Albert said. They came from some place out in Yoknapatawpha county, trying to get to Jefferson with it. It must have been like a piece of rotten cheese coming into an ant-hill, in that ramshackle wagon that Albert said folks were scared would fall all to pieces before they could get it out of town, with that home-made box and another fellow with a broken leg lying on a quilt on top of it, and the father and a little boy sitting on the seat and the marshal trying to make them get out of town.

"It's a public street," the man says. "I reckon we can stop to buy something same as airy other man. We got the money to pay for hit, and hit aint airy law that says a man cant spend his money where he wants."

They had stopped to buy some cement. The other

son was in Grummet's, trying to make Grummet break a sack and let him have ten cents' worth, and finally Grummet broke the sack to get him out. They wanted the cement to fix the fellow's broken leg, someway.

"Why, you'll kill him," the marshal said. "You'll cause him to lose his leg. You take him on to a doctor, and you get this thing buried soon as you can. Dont you know you're liable to jail for endangering the public health?"

"We're doing the best we can," the father said. Then he told a long tale about how they had to wait for the wagon to come back and how the bridge was washed away and how they went eight miles to another bridge and it was gone too so they came back and swum the ford and the mules got drowned and how they got another team and found that the road was washed out and they had to come clean around by Mottson, and then the one with the cement came back and told him to shut up.

"We'll be gone in a minute," he told the marshal.

"We never aimed to bother nobody," the father said.

"You take that fellow to a doctor," the marshal told the one with the cement.

"I reckon he's all right," he said.

"It aint that we're hard-hearted," the marshal said. "But I reckon you can tell yourself how it is."

"Sho," the other said. "We'll take out soon as Dewey Dell comes back. She went to deliver a package."

So they stood there with the folks backed off with handkerchiefs to their faces, until in a minute the girl came up with that newspaper package.

"Come on," the one with the cement said, "we've lost too much time." So they got in the wagon and went on. And when I went to supper it still seemed

like I could smell it. And the next day I met the marshal and I began to sniff and said,

"Smell anything?"

"I reckon they're in Jefferson by now," he said.

"Or in jail. Well, thank the Lord it's not our jail."

"That's a fact," he said.

Darl

"Here's a place," pa says. He pulls the team up and sits looking at the house. "We could get some water over yonder."

"All right," I say. "You'll have to borrow a bucket from them, Dewey Dell."

"God knows," pa says. "I wouldn't be beholden, God knows."

"If you see a good-sized can, you might bring it," I say. Dewey Dell gets down from the wagon, carrying the package. "You had more trouble than you expected, selling those cakes in Mottson," I say. How do our lives ravel out into the no-wind, no-sound, the weary gestures wearily recapitulant: echoes of old compulsions with no-hand on no-strings: in sunset we fall into furious attitudes, dead gestures of dolls. Cash broke his leg and now the sawdust is running out. He is bleeding to death is Cash.

"I wouldn't be beholden," pa says. "God knows."

"Then make some water yourself," I say. "We can use Cash's hat."

When Dewey Dell comes back the man comes with her. Then he stops and she comes on and he stands there and after a while he goes back to the house and stands on the porch, watching us.

"We better not try to lift him down," pa says. "We can fix it here."

"Do you want to be lifted down, Cash?" I say.

"Wont we get to Jefferson tomorrow?" he says. He is watching us, his eyes interrogatory, intent, and sad. "I can last it out."

"It'll be easier on you," pa says. "It'll keep it from rubbing together."

"I can last it," Cash says. "We'll lose time stopping."

"We done bought the cement, now," pa says.

"I could last it," Cash says. "It aint but one more day. It dont bother to speak of." He looks at us, his eyes wide in his thin gray face, questioning. "It sets up so," he says.

"We done bought it now," pa says.

I mix the cement in the can, stirring the slow water into the pale green thick coils. I bring the can to the wagon where Cash can see. He lies on his back, his thin profile in silhouette, ascetic and profound against the sky. "Does that look about right?" I say.

"You dont want too much water, or it wont work right," he says.

"Is this too much?"

"Maybe if you could get a little sand," he says. "It

aint but one more day," he says. "It dont bother me
none."

Vardaman goes back down the road to where we
crossed the branch and returns with sand. He pours
it slowly into the thick coiling in the can. I go to the
wagon again.

"Does that look all right?"

"Yes," Cash says. "I could have lasted. It dont
bother me none."

We loosen the splints and pour the cement over his
leg, slow.

"Watch out for it," Cash says. "Dont get none on it
if you can help."

"Yes," I say. Dewey Dell tears a piece of paper
from the package and wipes the cement from the top
of it as it drips from Cash's leg.

"How does that feel?"

"It feels fine," he says. "It's cold. It feels fine."

"If it'll just help you," pa says. "I asks your forgiveness. I never foreseen it no more than you."

"It feels fine," Cash says.

If you could just ravel out into time. That would
be nice. It would be nice if you could just ravel out
into time.

We replace the splints, the cords, drawing them
tight, the cement in thick pale green slow surges
among the cords, Cash watching us quietly with that
profound questioning look.

"That'll steady it," I say.

"Ay," Cash says. "I'm obliged."

Then we all turn on the wagon and watch him. He
is coming up the road behind us, wooden-backed,
wooden-faced, moving only from his hips down. He

comes up without a word, with his pale rigid eyes in his high sullen face, and gets into the wagon.

"Here's a hill," pa says. "I reckon you'll have to get out and walk."

Jewel comes back.

Vardaman

Darl and Jewel and Dewey Dell and I are walking up the hill, behind the wagon. Jewel came back. He came up the road and got into the wagon. He was walking. Jewel hasn't got a horse anymore. Jewel is my brother. Cash is my brother. Cash has a broken leg. We fixed Cash's leg so it doesn't hurt. Cash is my brother. Jewel is my brother too, but he hasn't got a broken leg.

Now there are five of them, tall in little tall black circles.

"Where do they stay at night, Darl?" I say. "When we stop at night in the barn, where do they stay?"

The hill goes off into the sky. Then the sun comes up from behind the hill and the mules and the wagon and pa walk on the sun. You cannot watch them, walking slow on the sun. In Jefferson it is red on the track behind the glass. The track goes shining round and round. Dewey Dell says so.

Tonight I am going to see where they stay while we are in the barn.

Darl

"Jewel," I say, "whose son are you?"

The breeze was setting up from the barn, so we put her under the apple tree, where the moonlight can dapple the apple tree upon the long slumbering flanks within which now and then she talks in little trickling bursts of secret and murmurous bubbling. I took Vardaman to listen. When we came up the cat leaped down from it and flicked away with silver claw and silver eye into the shadow.

"Your mother was a horse, but who was your father, Jewel?"

"You goddamn lying son of a bitch."

"Dont call me that," I say.

"You goddamn lying son of a bitch."

"Dont you call me that, Jewel." In the tall moonlight his eyes look like spots of white paper pasted on a high small football.

After supper Cash began to sweat a little. "It's getting a little hot," he said. "It was the sun shining on it all day, I reckon."

"You want some water poured on it?" we say. "Maybe that will ease it some."

"I'd be obliged," Cash said. "It was the sun shining on it, I reckon. I ought to thought and kept it covered."

"We ought to thought," we said. "You couldn't have suspicioned."

"I never noticed it getting hot," Cash said. "I ought to minded it."

So we poured the water over it. His leg and foot below the cement looked like they had been boiled. "Does that feel better?" we said.

"I'm obliged," Cash said. "It feels fine."

Dewey Dell wipes his face with the hem of her dress.

"See if you can get some sleep," we say.

"Sho," Cash says. "I'm right obliged. It feels fine now."

Jewel, I say, Who was your father, Jewel?

Goddamn you. Goddamn you.

Vardaman

She was under the apple tree and Darl and I go across the moon and the cat jumps down and runs and we can hear her inside the wood.

"Hear?" Darl says. "Put your ear close."

I put my ear close and I can hear her. Only I cant tell what she is saying.

"What is she saying, Darl?" I say. "Who is she talking to?"

"She's talking to God," Darl says. "She is calling on Him to help her."

"What does she want Him to do?" I say.

"She wants Him to hide her away from the sight of man," Darl says.

"Why does she want to hide her away from the sight of man, Darl?"

"So she can lay down her life," Darl says.

"Why does she want to lay down her life, Darl?"

"Listen," Darl says. We hear her. We hear her turn over on her side. "Listen," Darl says.

"She's turned over," I say. "She's looking at me through the wood."

"Yes," Darl says.

"How can she see through the wood, Darl?"

"Come," Darl says. "We must let her be quiet. Come."

"She cant see out there, because the holes are in the top," I say. "How can she see, Darl?"

"Let's go see about Cash," Darl says.

And I saw something Dewey Dell told me not to tell nobody

Cash is sick in his leg. We fixed his leg this afternoon, but he is sick in it again, lying on the bed. We pour water on his leg and then he feels fine.

"I feel fine," Cash says. "I'm obliged to you."

"Try to get some sleep," we say.

"I feel fine," Cash says. "I'm obliged to you."

And I saw something Dewey Dell told me not to tell nobody. It is not about pa and it is not about Cash and it is not about Jewel and it is not about Dewey Dell and it is not about me

Dewey Dell and I are going to sleep on the pallet. It is on the back porch, where we can see the barn, and the moon shines on half of the pallet and we will lie half in the white and half in the black, with the moonlight on our legs. And then I am going to see where they stay at night while we are in the barn. We are not in the barn tonight but I can see the barn and so I am going to find where they stay at night.

We lie on the pallet, with our legs in the moon.

"Look," I say, "my legs look black. Your legs look black, too."

"Go to sleep," Dewey Dell says.

Jefferson is a far piece.

"Dewey Dell."

"What."

"If it's not Christmas now, how will it be there?"

It goes round and round on the shining track. Then the track goes shining round and round.

"Will what be there?"

"That train. In the window."

"You go to sleep. You can see tomorrow if it's there."

Maybe Santa Claus wont know they are town boys.

"Dewey Dell."

"You go to sleep. He aint going to let none of them town boys have it."

It was behind the window, red on the track, the track shining round and round. It made my heart hurt. And then it was pa and Jewel and Darl and Mr Gillespie's boy. Mr Gillespie's boy's legs come down under his nightshirt. When he goes into the moon, his legs fuzz. They go on around the house toward the apple tree.

"What are they going to do, Dewey Dell?"

They went around the house toward the apple tree.

"I can smell her," I say. "Can you smell her, too?"

"Hush," Dewey Dell says. "The wind's changed. Go to sleep."

And so I am going to know where they stay at night soon. They come around the house, going across the yard in the moon, carrying her on their shoulders.

They carry her down to the barn, the moon shining
flat and quiet on her. Then they come back and go
into the house again. While they were in the moon,
Mr Gillespie's boy's legs fuzzed. And then I waited
and I said Dewey Dell? and then I waited and then
I went to find where they stay at night and I saw
something that Dewey Dell told me not to tell nobody.

Darl

Against the dark doorway he seems to materialise out
of darkness, lean as a race horse in his underclothes
in the beginning of the glare. He leaps to the ground
with on his face an expression of furious unbelief. He
has seen me without even turning his head or his eyes
in which the glare swims like two small torches.
"Come on," he says, leaping down the slope toward
the barn.

For an instant longer he runs silver in the moonlight, then he springs out like a flat figure cut leanly
from tin against an abrupt and soundless explosion
as the whole loft of the barn takes fire at once, as
though it had been stuffed with powder. The front,
the conical façade with the square orifice of doorway

broken only by the square squat shape of the coffin on the sawhorses like a cubistic bug, comes into relief. Behind me pa and Gillespie and Mack and Dewey Dell and Vardaman emerge from the house.

He pauses at the coffin, stooping, looking at me, his face furious. Overhead the flames sound like thunder; across us rushes a cool draft: there is no heat in it at all yet, and a handful of chaff lifts suddenly and sucks swiftly along the stalls where a horse is screaming. "Quick," I say; "the horses."

He glares a moment longer at me, then at the roof overhead, then he leaps toward the stall where the horse screams. It plunges and kicks, the sound of the crashing blows sucking up into the sound of the flames. They sound like an interminable train crossing an endless trestle. Gillespie and Mack pass me, in knee-length nightshirts, shouting, their voices thin and high and meaningless and at the same time profoundly wild and sad: ". . . cow . . . stall . . ." Gillespie's nightshirt rushes ahead of him on the draft, ballooning about his hairy thighs.

The stall door has swung shut. Jewel thrusts it back with his buttocks and he appears, his back arched, the muscles ridged through his garment as he drags the horse out by its head. In the glare its eyes roll with soft, fleet, wild opaline fire; its muscles bunch and run as it flings its head about, lifting Jewel clear of the ground. He drags it on, slowly, terrifically; again he gives me across his shoulder a single glare furious and brief. Even when they are clear of the barn the horse continues to fight and lash backward toward the doorway until Gillespie passes me, stark-naked, his nightshirt wrapped about the mule's head, and beats the maddened horse on out of the door.

Jewel returns, running; again he looks down at the coffin. But he comes on. "Where's cow?" he cries, passing me. I follow him. In the stall Mack is struggling with the other mule. When its head turns into the glare I can see the wild rolling of its eye too, but it makes no sound. It just stands there, watching Mack over its shoulder, swinging its hind quarters toward him whenever he approaches. He looks back at us, his eyes and mouth three round holes in his face on which the freckles look like English peas on a plate. His voice is thin, high, faraway.

"I cant do nothing . . ." It is as though the sound had been swept from his lips and up and away, speaking back to us from an immense distance of exhaustion. Jewel slides past us; the mule whirls and lashes out, but he has already gained its head. I lean to Mack's ear:

"Nightshirt. Around his head."

Mack stares at me. Then he rips the nightshirt off and flings it over the mule's head, and it becomes docile at once. Jewel is yelling at him: "Cow? Cow?"

"Back," Mack cries. "Last stall."

The cow watches us as we enter. She is backed into the corner, head lowered, still chewing though rapidly. But she makes no move. Jewel has paused, looking up, and suddenly we watch the entire floor to the loft dissolve. It just turns to fire; a faint litter of sparks rains down. He glances about. Back under the trough is a three legged milking stool. He catches it up and swings it into the planking of the rear wall. He splinters a plank, then another, a third; we tear the fragments away. While we are stooping at the opening something charges into us from behind. It is the cow; with a single whistling breath she rushes between us and through the gap and into the outer glare, her tail erect and rigid as a broom nailed upright to the end of her spine.

Jewel turns back into the barn. "Here," I say; "Jewel!" I grasp at him; he strikes my hand down. "You fool," I say, "dont you see you cant make it back yonder?" The hallway looks like a searchlight turned into rain. "Come on," I say, "around this way."

When we are through the gap he begins to run. "Jewel," I say, running. He darts around the corner. When I reach it he has almost reached the next one, running against the glare like that figure cut from tin. Pa and Gillespie and Mack are some distance away, watching the barn, pink against the darkness where for the time the moonlight has been vanquished. "Catch him!" I cry; "stop him!"

When I reach the front, he is struggling with Gillespie; the one lean in underclothes, the other stark naked. They are like two figures in a Greek frieze, isolated out of all reality by the red glare. Before I can reach them he has struck Gillespie to the ground and turned and run back into the barn.

The sound of it has become quite peaceful now, like the sound of the river did. We watch through the dissolving proscenium of the doorway as Jewel runs crouching to the far end of the coffin and stoops to it. For an instant he looks up and out at us through the rain of burning hay like a portiere of flaming beads, and I can see his mouth shape as he calls my name.

"Jewel!" Dewey Dell cries; "Jewel!" It seems to me that I now hear the accumulation of her voice through the last five minutes, and I hear her scuffling and struggling as pa and Mack hold her, screaming "Jewel! Jewel!" But he is no longer looking at us. We see his shoulders strain as he upends the coffin and slides it single-handed from the sawhorses. It looms unbelievably tall, hiding him: I would not have believed that Addie Bundren would have needed that much room to lie comfortable in; for another instant it stands upright while the sparks rain on it in scattering bursts as though they engendered other sparks from the contact. Then it topples forward, gaining momentum, revealing Jewel and the sparks raining on him too in engendering gusts, so that he appears to be enclosed in a thin nimbus of fire. Without stopping it overends and rears again, pauses, then crashes slowly forward and through the curtain. This time Jewel is riding upon it, clinging to it, until it crashes down and flings him forward and clear and Mack leaps forward into a thin smell of scorching meat and slaps at the widening crimson-edged holes that bloom like flowers in his undershirt.

Vardaman

When I went to find where they stay at night, I saw something They said, "Where is Darl? Where did Darl go?"

They carried her back under the apple tree.

The barn was still red, but it wasn't a barn now. It was sunk down, and the red went swirling up. The barn went swirling up in little red pieces, against the sky and the stars so that the stars moved backward.

And then Cash was still awake. He turned his head from side to side, with sweat on his face.

"Do you want some more water on it, Cash?" Dewey Dell said.

Cash's leg and foot turned black. We held the lamp and looked at Cash's foot and leg where it was black.

"Your foot looks like a nigger's foot, Cash," I said.

"I reckon we'll have to bust it off," pa said.

"What in the tarnation you put it on there for," Mr Gillespie said.

"I thought it would steady it some," pa said. "I just aimed to help him."

They got the flat iron and the hammer. Dewey Dell held the lamp. They had to hit it hard. And then Cash went to sleep.

"He's asleep now," I said. "It cant hurt him while he's asleep."

It just cracked. It wouldn't come off.

"It'll take the hide, too," Mr Gillespie said. "Why in the tarnation you put it on there. Didn't none of you think to grease his leg first?"

"I just aimed to help him," pa said. "It was Darl put it on."

"Where is Darl?" they said.

"Didn't none of you have more sense than that?" Mr Gillespie said. "I'd a thought he would, anyway."

Jewel was lying on his face. His back was red. Dewey Dell put the medicine on it. The medicine was made out of butter and soot, to draw out the fire. Then his back was black.

"Does it hurt, Jewel?" I said. "Your back looks like a nigger's, Jewel," I said. Cash's foot and leg looked like a nigger's. Then they broke it off. Cash's leg bled.

"You go on back and lay down," Dewey Dell said. "You ought to be asleep."

"Where is Darl?" they said.

He is out there under the apple tree with her, lying on her. He is there so the cat wont come back. I said, "Are you going to keep the cat away, Darl?"

The moonlight dappled on him too. On her it was still, but on Darl it dappled up and down.

"You needn't to cry," I said. "Jewel got her out. You needn't to cry, Darl."

The barn is still red. It used to be redder than this. Then it went swirling, making the stars run backward without falling. It hurt my heart like the train did.

When I went to find where they stay at night, I saw something that Dewey Dell says I mustn't never tell nobody

Darl

We have been passing the signs for some time now: the drugstores, the clothing stores, the patent medicine and the garages and cafes, and the mile-boards diminishing, becoming more starkly reaccruent: 3 mi. 2 mi. From the crest of a hill, as we get into the wagon again, we can see the smoke low and flat, seemingly unmoving in the unwinded afternoon.

"Is that it, Darl?" Vardaman says. "Is that Jefferson?" He too has lost flesh; like ours, his face has an expression strained, dreamy, and gaunt.

"Yes," I say. He lifts his head and looks at the sky. High against it they hang in narrowing circles, like the smoke, with an outward semblance of form and purpose, but with no inference of motion, progress or retrograde. We mount the wagon again where Cash lies on the box, the jagged shards of cement cracked about his leg. The shabby mules droop rattling and clanking down the hill.

"We'll have to take him to the doctor," pa says. "I reckon it aint no way around it." The back of Jewel's shirt, where it touches him, stains slow and black with grease. Life was created in the valleys. It blew up onto the hills on the old terrors, the old lusts, the old despairs. That's why you must walk up the hills so you can ride down.

Dewey Dell sits on the seat, the newspaper package on her lap. When we reach the foot of the hill where the road flattens between close walls of trees, she begins to look about quietly from one side of the road to the other. At last she says,

"I got to stop."

Pa looks at her, his shabby profile that of anticipant and disgruntled annoyance. He does not check the team. "What for?"

"I got to go to the bushes," Dewey Dell says.

Pa does not check the team. "Cant you wait till we get to town? It aint over a mile now."

"Stop," Dewey Dell says. "I got to go to the bushes."

Pa stops in the middle of the road and we watch Dewey Dell descend, carrying the package. She does not look back.

"Why not leave your cakes here?" I say. "We'll watch them."

She descends steadily, not looking at us.

"How would she know where to go if she waited till we get to town?" Vardaman says. "Where would you go to do it in town, Dewey Dell?"

She lifts the package down and turns and disappears among the trees and undergrowth.

"Dont be no longer than you can help," pa says. "We aint got no time to waste." She does not answer. After a while we cannot hear her even. "We ought to done like Armstid and Gillespie said and sent word to town and had it dug and ready," he said.

"Why didn't you?" I say. "You could have telephoned."

"What for?" Jewel says. "Who the hell cant dig a hole in the ground?"

A car comes over the hill. It begins to sound the horn, slowing. It runs along the roadside in low gear, the outside wheels in the ditch, and passes us and goes on. Vardaman watches it until it is out of sight.

"How far is it now, Darl?" he says.

"Not far," I say.

"We ought to done it," pa says. "I just never wanted to be beholden to none except her flesh and blood."

"Who the hell cant dig a damn hole in the ground?" Jewel says.

"It aint respectful, talking that way about her grave," pa says. "You all dont know what it is. You never pure loved her, none of you." Jewel does not answer. He sits a little stiffly erect, his body arched away from his shirt. His high-colored jaw juts.

Dewey Dell returns. We watch her emerge from the bushes, carrying the package, and climb into the wagon. She now wears her Sunday dress, her beads, her shoes and stockings.

"I thought I told you to leave them clothes to home," pa says. She does not answer, does not look at us. She sets the package in the wagon and gets in. The wagon moves on.

"How many more hills now, Darl?" Vardaman says.

"Just one," I say. "The next one goes right up into town."

This hill is red sand, bordered on either hand by negro cabins; against the sky ahead the massed telephone lines run, and the clock on the courthouse lifts among the trees. In the sand the wheels whisper, as though the very earth would hush our entry. We descend as the hill commences to rise.

We follow the wagon, the whispering wheels, passing the cabins where faces come suddenly to the doors, white-eyed. We hear sudden voices, ejaculant. Jewel has been looking from side to side; now his head turns forward and I can see his ears taking on a still deeper tone of furious red. Three negroes walk beside the road ahead of us; ten feet ahead of them a white man walks. When we pass the negroes their heads turn suddenly with that expression of shock and instinctive outrage. "Great God," one says; "what they got in that wagon?"

Jewel whirls. "Son of a bitches," he says. As he does so he is abreast of the white man, who has paused. It is as though Jewel had gone blind for the moment, for it is the white man toward whom he whirls.

"Darl!" Cash says from the wagon. I grasp at Jewel. The white man has fallen back a pace, his face still slack-jawed; then his jaw tightens, claps to. Jewel leans above him, his jaw muscles gone white.

"What did you say?" he says.

"Here," I say. "He dont mean anything, mister. Jewel," I say. When I touch him he swings at the man. I grasp his arm; we struggle. Jewel has never looked at me. He is trying to free his arm. When I see the man again he has an open knife in his hand.

"Hold up, mister," I say; "I've got him. Jewel," I say.

"Thinks because he's a goddamn town fellow," Jewel says, panting, wrenching at me. "Son of a bitch," he says.

The man moves. He begins to edge around me, watching Jewel, the knife low against his flank. "Cant no man call me that," he says. Pa has got down, and Dewey Dell is holding Jewel, pushing at him. I release him and face the man.

"Wait," I say. "He dont mean nothing. He's sick; got burned in a fire last night, and he aint himself."

"Fire or no fire," the man says, "cant no man call me that."

"He thought you said something to him," I say.

"I never said nothing to him. I never see him before."

"Fore God," pa says; "fore God."

"I know," I say. "He never meant anything. He'll take it back."

"Let him take it back, then."

"Put up your knife, and he will."

The man looks at me. He looks at Jewel. Jewel is quiet now.

"Put up your knife," I say.

The man shuts the knife.

"Fore God," pa says. "Fore God."

"Tell him you didn't mean anything, Jewel," I say.

"I thought he said something," Jewel says. "Just because he's—"

"Hush," I say. "Tell him you didn't mean it."

"I didn't mean it," Jewel says.

"He better not," the man says. "Calling me a—"

"Do you think he's afraid to call you that?" I say.

The man looks at me. "I never said that," he said.

"Dont think it, neither," Jewel says.

"Shut up," I say. "Come on. Drive on, pa."

The wagon moves. The man stands watching us. Jewel does not look back. "Jewel would a whipped him," Vardaman says.

We approach the crest, where the street runs, where cars go back and forth; the mules haul the wagon up and onto the crest and the street. Pa stops them. The street runs on ahead, where the square opens and the monument stands before the courthouse. We mount again while the heads turn with that expression which we know; save Jewel. He does not get on, even though the wagon has started again. "Get in, Jewel," I say. "Come on. Let's get away from here." But he does not get in. Instead he sets his foot on the turning hub of the rear wheel, one hand grasping the stanchion, and with the hub turning smoothly under his sole he lifts the other foot and squats there, staring straight ahead, motionless, lean, wooden-backed, as though carved squatting out of the lean wood.

Cash

It wasn't nothing else to do. It was either send him to Jackson, or have Gillespie sue us, because he knowed some way that Darl set fire to it. I dont know how he knowed, but he did. Vardaman see him do it, but he swore he never told nobody but Dewey Dell and that she told him not to tell nobody. But Gillespie knowed it. But he would a suspicioned it sooner or later. He could have done it that night just watching the way Darl acted.

And so pa said, "I reckon there aint nothing else to do," and Jewel said,

"You want to fix him now?"

"Fix him?" pa said.

"Catch him and tie him up," Jewel said. "Goddamn

ahead," Darl said. "Dont you want to go to Peabody's now, Cash?"

"Go on," I said. "It feels right easy now. It's best to get things done in the right place."

"If it was just dug," pa says. "We forgot our spade, too."

"Yes," Darl said. "I'll go to the hardware store. We'll have to buy one."

"It'll cost money," pa says.

"Do you begrudge her it?" Darl says.

"Go on and get a spade," Jewel said. "Here. Give me the money."

But pa didn't stop. "I reckon we can get a spade," he said. "I reckon there are Christians here." So Darl set still and we went on, with Jewel squatting on the tail-gate, watching the back of Darl's head. He looked like one of these bull dogs, one of these dogs that dont bark none, squatting against the rope, watching the thing he was waiting to jump at.

He set that way all the time we was in front of Mrs Bundren's house, hearing the music, watching the back of Darl's head with them hard white eyes of hisn.

The music was playing in the house. It was one of them graphophones. It was natural as a music-band.

"Do you want to go to Peabody's?" Darl said. "They can wait here and tell pa, and I'll drive you to Peabody's and come back for them."

"No," I said. It was better to get her underground, now we was this close, just waiting until pa borrowed the shovel. He drove along the street until we could hear the music.

"Maybe they got one here," he said. He pulled up at Mrs Bundren's. It was like he knowed. Sometimes I think that if a working man could see work as far ahead as a lazy man can see laziness. So he stopped there like he knowed, before that little new house, where the music was. We waited there, hearing it. I believe I could have dickered Suratt down to five dollars on that one of his. It's a comfortable thing, music is. "Maybe they got one here," pa says.

"You want Jewel to go," Darl says, "or do you reckon I better?"

"I reckon I better," pa says. He got down and went up the path and around the house to the back. The music stopped, then it started again.

"He'll get it, too," Darl said.

"Ay," I said. It was just like he knowed, like he could see through the walls and into the next ten minutes.

Only it was more than ten minutes. The music stopped and never commenced again for a good spell, where her and pa was talking at the back. We waited in the wagon.

"You let me take you back to Peabody's," Darl said.

"No," I said. "We'll get her underground."

"If he ever gets back," Jewel said. He begun to cuss. He started to get down from the wagon. "I'm going," he said.

Then we saw pa coming back. He had two spades, coming around the house. He laid them in the wagon and got in and we went on. The music never started again. Pa was looking back at the house. He kind of lifted his hand a little and I saw the shade pulled back a little at the window and her face in it.

But the curiousest thing was Dewey Dell. It surprised me. I see all the while how folks could say he was queer, but that was the very reason couldn't nobody hold it personal. It was like he was outside of it

too, same as you, and getting mad at it would be kind
of like getting mad at a mud-puddle that splashed
you when you stepped in it. And then I always kind
of had a idea that him and Dewey Dell kind of knowed
things betwixt them. If I'd a said it was ere a one of
us she liked better than ere a other, I'd a said it was
Darl. But when we got it filled and covered and drove
out the gate and turned into the lane where them fellows was waiting, when they come out and come on
him and he jerked back, it was Dewey Dell that was
on him before even Jewel could get at him. And then
I believed I knowed how Gillespie knowed about how
his barn taken fire.

She hadn't said a word, hadn't even looked at him,
but when them fellows told him what they wanted and
that they had come to get him and he throwed back,
she jumped on him like a wild cat so that one of the
fellows had to quit and hold her and her scratching
and clawing at him like a wild cat, while the other
one and pa and Jewel throwed Darl down and held
him lying on his back, looking up at me.

"I thought you would have told me," he said. "I
never thought you wouldn't have."

"Darl," I said. But he fought again, him and Jewel
and the fellow, and the other one holding Dewey Dell
and Vardaman yelling and Jewel saying,

"Kill him. Kill the son of a bitch."

It was bad so. It was bad. A fellow cant get away
from a shoddy job. He cant do it. I tried to tell him,
but he just said, "I thought you'd a told me. It's not
that I," he said, then he begun to laugh. The other
fellow pulled Jewel off of him and he sat there on the
ground, laughing.

I tried to tell him. If I could have just moved, even

set up. But I tried to tell him and he quit laughing, looking up at me.

"Do you want me to go?" he said.

"It'll be better for you," I said. "Down there it'll be quiet, with none of the bothering and such. It'll be better for you, Darl," I said.

"Better," he said. He begun to laugh again. "Better," he said. He couldn't hardly say it for laughing. He sat on the ground and us watching him, laughing and laughing. It was bad. It was bad so. I be durn if I could see anything to laugh at. Because there just aint nothing justifies the deliberate destruction of what a man has built with his own sweat and stored the fruit of his sweat into.

But I aint so sho that ere a man has the right to say what is crazy and what aint. It's like there was a fellow in every man that's done a-past the sanity or the insanity, that watches the sane and the insane doings of that man with the same horror and the same astonishment.

Peabody

I said, "I reckon a man in a tight might let Bill Varner patch him up like a damn mule, but I be damned if the man that'd let Anse Bundren treat him with raw cement aint got more spare legs than I have."

"They just aimed to ease hit some," he said.

"Aimed, hell," I said. "What in hell did Armstid mean by even letting them put you on that wagon again?"

"Hit was gittin right noticeable," he said. "We never had time to wait." I just looked at him. "Hit never bothered me none," he said.

"Dont you lie there and try to tell me you rode six days on a wagon without springs, with a broken leg and it never bothered you."

"It never bothered me much," he said.

"You mean, it never bothered Anse much," I said. "No more than it bothered him to throw that poor devil down in the public street and handcuff him like a damn murderer. Dont tell me. And dont tell me it aint going to bother you to lose sixty-odd square inches of skin to get that concrete off. And dont tell me it aint going to bother you to have to limp around on one short leg for the balance of your life—if you walk at all again. Concrete," I said. "God Amighty, why didn't Anse carry you to the nearest sawmill and stick your leg in the saw? That would have cured it. Then you all could have stuck his head into the saw and cured a whole family . . . Where is Anse, anyway? What's he up to now?"

"He's takin back them spades he borrowed," he said.

"That's right," I said. "Of course he'd have to borrow a spade to bury his wife with. Unless he could borrow a hole in the ground. Too bad you all didn't put him in it too . . . Does that hurt?"

"Not to speak of," he said, and the sweat big as marbles running down his face and his face about the color of blotting paper.

"Course not," I said. "About next summer you can hobble around fine on this leg. Then it wont bother you, not to speak of . . . If you had anything you could call luck, you might say it was lucky this is the same leg you broke before," I said.

"Hit's what paw says," he said.

MacGowan

It happened I am back of the prescription case, pouring up some chocolate sauce, when Jody comes back and says, "Say, Skeet, there's a woman up front that wants to see the doctor and when I said What doctor you want to see, she said she wants to see the doctor that works here and when I said There aint any doctor works here, she just stood there, looking back this way."

"What kind of a woman is it?" I says. "Tell her to go upstairs to Alford's office."

"Country woman," he says.

"Send her to the courthouse," I says. "Tell her all the doctors have gone to Memphis to a Barbers' Convention."

"All right," he says, going away. "She looks pretty good for a country girl," he says.

"Wait," I says. He waited and I went and peeped through the crack. But I couldn't tell nothing except she had a good leg against the light. "Is she young, you say?" I says.

"She looks like a pretty hot mamma, for a country girl," he says.

"Take this," I says, giving him the chocolate. I took off my apron and went up there. She looked pretty good. One of them black eyed ones that look like she'd as soon put a knife in you as not if you two-timed her. She looked pretty good. There wasn't nobody else in the store; it was dinner time.

"What can I do for you?" I says.

"Are you the doctor?" she says.

"Sure," I says. She quit looking at me and was kind of looking around.

"Can we go back yonder?" she says.

It was just a quarter past twelve, but I went and told Jody to kind of watch out and whistle if the old man come in sight, because he never got back before one.

"You better lay off of that," Jody says. "He'll fire your stern out of here so quick you cant wink."

"He dont never get back before one," I says. "You can see him go into the postoffice. You keep your eye peeled, now, and give me a whistle."

"What you going to do?" he says.

"You keep your eye out. I'll tell you later."

"Aint you going to give me no seconds on it?" he says.

"What the hell do you think this is?" I says; "a stud-farm? You watch out for him. I'm going into conference."

So I go on to the back. I stopped at the glass and smoothed my hair, then I went behind the prescription case, where she was waiting. She is looking at the medicine cabinet, then she looks at me.

"Now, madam," I says; "what is your trouble?"

"It's the female trouble," she says, watching me. "I got the money," she says.

"Ah," I says. "Have you got female troubles or do you want female troubles? If so, you come to the right doctor." Them country people. Half the time they dont know what they want, and the balance of the time they cant tell it to you. The clock said twenty past twelve.

"No," she says.

"No which?" I says.

"I aint had it," she says. "That's it." She looked at me. "I got the money," she says.

So I knew what she was talking about.

"Oh," I says. "You got something in your belly you wish you didn't have." She looks at me. "You wish you had a little more or a little less, huh?"

"I got the money," she says. "He said I could git something at the drugstore for hit."

"Who said so?" I says.

"He did," she says, looking at me.

"You dont want to call no names," I says. "The one that put the acorn in your belly? He the one that told you?" She dont say nothing. "You aint married, are you?" I says. I never saw no ring. But like as not, they aint heard yet out there that they use rings.

"I got the money," she says. She showed it to me, tied up in her handkerchief: a ten spot.

"I'll swear you have," I says. "He give it to you?"

"Yes," she says.

"Which one?" I says. She looks at me. "Which one of them give it to you?"

"It aint but one," she says. She looks at me.

"Go on," I says. She dont say nothing. The trouble about the cellar is, it aint but one way out and that's back up the inside stairs. The clock says twenty-five to one. "A pretty girl like you," I says.

She looks at me. She begins to tie the money back up in the handkerchief. "Excuse me a minute," I says. I go around the prescription case. "Did you hear about that fellow sprained his ear?" I says. "After that he couldn't even hear a belch."

"You better get her out from back there before the old man comes," Jody says.

"If you'll stay up there in front where he pays you to stay, he wont catch nobody but me," I says.

He goes on, slow, toward the front. "What you doing to her, Skeet?" he says.

"I cant tell you," I says. "It wouldn't be ethical. You go on up there and watch."

"Say, Skeet," he says.

"Ah, go on," I says. "I aint doing nothing but filling a prescription."

"He may not do nothing about that woman back there, but if he finds you monkeying with that prescription case, he'll kick your stern clean down them cellar stairs."

"My stern has been kicked by bigger bastards than him," I says. "Go back and watch out for him, now."

So I come back. The clock said fifteen to one. She is tying the money in the handkerchief. "You aint the doctor," she says.

"Sure I am," I says. She watches me. "Is it because I look too young, or am I too handsome?" I says. "We used to have a bunch of old water-jointed doctors here," I says; "Jefferson used to be a kind of Old Doctors' Home for them. But business started falling off and folks stayed so well until one day they found out that the women wouldn't never get sick at all. So they run all the old doctors out and got us young goodlooking ones that the women would like and then the women begun to get sick again and so business picked up. They're doing that all over the country. Hadn't you heard about it? Maybe it's because you aint never needed a doctor."

"I need one now," she says.

"And you come to the right one," I says. "I already told you that."

"Have you got something for it?" she says. "I got the money."

"Well," I says, "of course a doctor has to learn all sorts of things while he's learning to roll calomel; he cant help himself. But I dont know about your trouble."

"He told me I could get something. He told me I could get it at the drugstore."

"Did he tell you the name of it?" I says. "You better go back and ask him."

She quit looking at me, kind of turning the handkerchief in her hands. "I got to do something," she says.

"How bad do you want to do something?" I says. She looks at me. "Of course, a doctor learns all sorts of things folks dont think he knows. But he aint supposed to tell all he knows. It's against the law."

Up front Jody says, "Skeet."

"Excuse me a minute," I says. I went up front. "Do you see him?" I says.

"Aint you done yet?" he says. "Maybe you better come up here and watch and let me do that consulting."

"Maybe you'll lay a egg," I says. I come back. She is looking at me. "Of course you realise that I could be put in the penitentiary for doing what you want," I says. "I would lose my license and then I'd have to go to work. You realise that?"

"I aint got but ten dollars," she says. "I could bring the rest next month, maybe."

"Pooh," I says, "ten dollars? You see, I cant put no price on my knowledge and skill. Certainly not for no little paltry sawbuck."

She looks at me. She dont even blink. "What you want, then?"

The clock said four to one. So I decided I better get her out. "You guess three times and then I'll show you," I says.

She dont even blink her eyes. "I got to do something," she says. She looks behind her and around, then she looks toward the front. "Gimme the medicine first," she says.

"You mean, you're ready to right now?" I says. "Here?"

"Gimme the medicine first," she says.

So I took a graduated glass and kind of turned my back to her and picked out a bottle that looked all right, because a man that would keep poison setting around in a unlabelled bottle ought to be in jail, anyway. It smelled like turpentine. I poured some into the glass and give it to her. She smelled it, looking at me across the glass.

"Hit smells like turpentine," she says.

"Sure," I says. "That's just the beginning of the treatment. You come back at ten oclock tonight and I'll give you the rest of it and perform the operation."

"Operation?" she says.

"It wont hurt you. You've had the same operation before. Ever hear about the hair of the dog?"

She looks at me. "Will it work?" she says.

"Sure it'll work. If you come back and get it."

So she drunk whatever it was without batting a eye, and went out. I went up front.

"Didn't you get it?" Jody says.

"Get what?" I says.

"Ah, come on," he says. "I aint going to try to beat your time."

"Oh, her," I says. "She just wanted a little medicine. She's got a bad case of dysentery and she's a little ashamed about mentioning it with a stranger there."

It was my night, anyway, so I helped the old bastard check up and I got his hat on him and got him out of the store by eight-thirty. I went as far as the corner with him and watched him until he passed under two street lamps and went on out of sight. Then I come back to the store and waited until nine-thirty and turned out the front lights and locked the door and left just one light burning at the back, and I went back and put some talcum powder into six capsules and kind of cleared up the cellar and then I was all ready.

She come in just at ten, before the clock had done striking. I let her in and she come in, walking fast. I looked out the door, but there wasn't nobody but a boy in overalls sitting on the curb. "You want something?" I says. He never said nothing, just looking at me. I locked the door and turned off the light and went on back. She was waiting. She didn't look at me now.

"Where is it?" she said.

I gave her the box of capsules. She held the box in her hand, looking at the capsules.

"Are you sure it'll work?" she says.

"Sure," I says. "When you take the rest of the treatment."

"Where do I take it?" she says.

"Down in the cellar," I says.

Vardaman

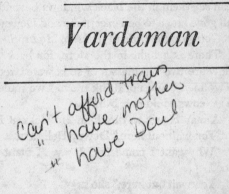

Can't afford train
" have mother
× have Darl

Now it is wider and lighter, but the stores are dark because they have all gone home. The stores are dark, but the lights pass on the windows when we pass. The lights are in the trees around the courthouse. They roost in the trees, but the courthouse is dark. The clock on it looks four ways, because it is not dark. The moon is not dark too. Not very dark. *Darl he went to Jackson is my brother Darl is my brother* Only it was over that way, shining on the track.

"Let's go that way, Dewey Dell," I say.

"What for?" Dewey Dell says. The track went shining around the window, it red on the track. But she

Relates Darl & the train

said he would not sell it to the town boys. "But it will be there Christmas," Dewey Dell says. "You'll have to wait till then, when he brings it back."

Darl went to Jackson. Lots of people didn't go to Jackson. Darl is my brother. My brother is going to Jackson

While we walk the lights go around, roosting in the trees. On all sides it is the same. They go around the courthouse and then you cannot see them. But you can see them in the black windows beyond. They have all gone home to bed except me and Dewey Dell.

Going on the train to Jackson. My brother

There is a light in the store, far back. In the window are two big glasses of soda water, red and green. Two men could not drink them. Two mules could not. Two cows could not. *Darl*

A man comes to the door. He looks at Dewey Dell.

"You wait out here," Dewey Dell says.

"Why cant I come in?" I say. "I want to come in, too."

"You wait out here," she says.

"All right," I say.

Dewey Dell goes in.

Darl is my brother. Darl went crazy

The walk is harder than sitting on the ground. He is in the open door. He looks at me. "You want something?" he says. His head is slick. Jewel's head is slick sometimes. Cash's head is not slick. *Darl he went to Jackson my brother Darl* In the street he ate a banana. *Wouldn't you rather have bananas? Dewey Dell said. You wait till Christmas. It'll be there then. Then you can see it. So we are going to have some bananas. We are going to have a bag full, me and Dewey Dell. He* locks the door. Dewey Dell is inside. Then the light winks out.

He went to Jackson. He went crazy and went to Jackson both. Lots of people didn't go crazy. Pa and Cash and Jewel and Dewey Dell and me didn't go crazy. We never did go crazy. We didn't go to Jackson either. Darl

I hear the cow a long time, clopping   on the street. Then she comes into the square. She goes across the square, her head down   clopping   . She lows. There was nothing in the square before she lowed, but it wasn't empty. Now it is empty after she lowed. She goes on, clopping   . She lows. *My brother is Darl. He went to Jackson on the train. He didn't go on the train to go crazy. He went crazy in our wagon. Darl* She has been in there a long time. And the cow is gone too. A long time. She has been in there longer than the cow was. But not as long as empty. *Darl is my brother. My brother Darl*

Dewey Dell comes out. She looks at me.

"Let's go around that way now," I say.

She looks at me. "It aint going to work," she says. "That son of a bitch."

"What aint going to work, Dewey Dell?"

"I just know it wont," she says. She is not looking at anything. "I just know it."

"Let's go that way," I say.

"We got to go back to the hotel. It's late. We got to slip back in."

"Cant we go by and see, anyway?"

"Hadn't you rather have bananas? Hadn't you rather?"

"All right." *My brother he went crazy and he went to Jackson too. Jackson is further away than crazy*

"It wont work," Dewey Dell says. "I just know it wont."

"What wont work?" I say. *He had to get on the train to go to Jackson. I have not been on the train, but Darl has been on the train. Darl. Darl is my brother. Darl. Darl*

Darl

Darl has gone to Jackson. They put him on the train, laughing, down the long car laughing, the heads turning like the heads of owls when he passed. "What are you laughing at?" I said.

"Yes yes yes yes yes."

Two men put him on the train. They wore mismatched coats, bulging behind over their right hip pockets. Their necks were shaved to a hairline, as though the recent and simultaneous barbers had had a chalk-line like Cash's. "Is it the pistols you're laughing at?" I said. "Why do you laugh?" I said. "Is it because you hate the sound of laughing?"

They pulled two seats together so Darl could sit by the window to laugh. One of them sat beside him,

the other sat on the seat facing him, riding backward.
One of them had to ride backward because the state's
money has a face to each backside and a backside to
each face, and they are riding on the state's money
which is incest. A nickel has a woman on one side and
a buffalo on the other; two faces and no back. I dont
know what that is. Darl had a little spy-glass he got
in France at the war. In it it had a woman and a pig
with two backs and no face. I know what that is. "Is
that why you are laughing, Darl?"

"Yes yes yes yes yes yes." (crazy Darl)

The wagon stands on the square, hitched, the mules
motionless, the reins wrapped about the seat-spring,
the back of the wagon toward the courthouse. It looks
no different from a hundred other wagons there;
Jewel standing beside it and looking up the street like
any other man in town that day, yet there is something different, distinctive. There is about it that un-
mistakable air of definite and imminent departure
that trains have, perhaps due to the fact that Dewey
Dell and Vardaman on the seat and Cash on a pallet
in the wagon bed are eating bananas from a paper
bag. "Is that why you are laughing, Darl?"

Darl is our brother, our brother Darl. Our brother
Darl in a cage in Jackson where, his grimed hands lying light in the quiet interstices, looking out he foams.

"Yes yes yes yes yes yes yes yes."

Darl is talking with himself.
Split himself
– objective
– subjective

Dewey Dell

When he saw the money I said, "It's not my money, it doesn't belong to me."

"Whose is it, then?"

"It's Cora Tull's money. It's Mrs Tull's. I sold the cakes for it."

"Ten dollars for two cakes?"

"Dont you touch it. It's not mine."

"You never had them cakes. It's a lie. It was them Sunday clothes you had in that package."

"Dont you touch it! If you take it you are a thief."

"My own daughter accuses me of being a thief. My own daughter."

"Pa. Pa."

"I have fed you and sheltered you. I give you love

and care, yet my own daughter, the daughter of my dead wife, calls me a thief over her mother's grave."

"It's not mine, I tell you. If it was, God knows you could have it."

"Where did you get ten dollars?"

"Pa. Pa."

"You wont tell me. Did you come by it so shameful you dare not?"

"It's not mine, I tell you. Cant you understand it's not mine?"

"It's not like I wouldn't pay it back. But she calls her own father a thief."

D.D. "I cant, I tell you. I tell you it's not my money. God knows you could have it."

"I wouldn't take it. My own born daughter that has et my food for seventeen years, begrudges me the loan of ten dollars."

"It's not mine. I cant."

"Whose is it, then?"

"It was give to me. To buy something with."

"To buy what with?"

"Pa. Pa."

"It's just a loan. God knows, I hate for my blooden children to reproach me. But I give them what was mine without stint. Cheerful I give them, without stint. And now they deny me. Addie. It was lucky for you you died, Addie."

"Pa. Pa."

"God knows it is."

He took the money and went out.

Cash

So when we stopped there to borrow the shovels we heard the graphophone playing in the house, and so when we got done with the shovels pa says, "I reckon I better take them back."

So we went back to the house. "We better take Cash on to Peabody's," Jewel said.

"It wont take but a minute," pa said. He got down from the wagon. The music was not playing now.

"Let Vardaman do it," Jewel said. "He can do it in half the time you can. Or here, you let me—"

"I reckon I better do it," pa says. "Long as it was me that borrowed them."

So we set in the wagon, but the music wasn't playing now. I reckon it's a good thing we aint got ere a one of them. I reckon I wouldn't never get no work done a-tall for listening to it. I dont know if a little music aint about the nicest thing a fellow can have. Seems like when he comes in tired of a night, it aint nothing could rest him like having a little music played and him resting. I have see them that shuts up like a hand-grip, with a handle and all, so a fellow can carry it with him wherever he wants.

"What you reckon he's doing?" Jewel says. "I could a toted them shovels back and forth ten times by now."

"Let him take his time," I said. "He aint as spry as you, remember."

"Why didn't he let me take them back, then? We got to get your leg fixed up so we can start home to-morrow."

"We got plenty of time," I said. "I wonder what them machines costs on the installment."

"Installment of what?" Jewel said. "What you got to buy it with?"

"A fellow cant tell," I said. "I could a bought that one from Suratt for five dollars, I believe."

And so pa come back and we went to Peabody's. While we was there pa said he was going to the barbershop and get a shave. And so that night he said he had some business to tend to, kind of looking away from us while he said it, with his hair combed wet and slick and smelling sweet with perfume, but I said leave him be; I wouldn't mind hearing a little more of that music myself.

And so next morning he was gone again, then he come back and told us to get hitched up and ready to take out and he would meet us and when they was gone he said,

"I dont reckon you got no more money."

"Peabody just give me enough to pay the hotel with," I said. "We dont need nothing else, do we?"

"No," pa said; "no. We dont need nothing." He stood there, not looking at me.

"If it is something we got to have, I reckon maybe Peabody," I said.

"No," he said; "it aint nothing else. You all wait for me at the corner."

So Jewel got the team and come for me and they fixed me a pallet in the wagon and we drove across the square to the corner where pa said, and we was waiting there in the wagon, with Dewey Dell and Vardaman eating bananas, when we see them coming up the street. Pa was coming along with that kind of daresome and hangdog look all at once like when he has been up to something he knows ma aint going to like, carrying a grip in his hand, and Jewel says,

"Who's that?"

Then we see it wasn't the grip that made him look different; it was his face, and Jewel says, "He got them teeth."

It was a fact. It made him look a foot taller, kind of holding his head up, hangdog and proud too, and then we see her behind him, carrying the other grip—a kind of duck-shaped woman all dressed up, with them kind of hard-looking pop eyes like she was daring ere a man to say nothing. And there we set watching them, with Dewey Dell's and Vardaman's mouth half open and half-et bananas in their hands and her coming around from behind pa, looking at us like she dared ere a man. And then I see that the grip she was carrying was one of them little graphophones. It was for a fact, all shut up as pretty as a picture, and everytime a new record would come from the mail order and us setting in the house in the winter, listening to it, I would think what a shame Darl couldn't be to enjoy it too. But it is better so for him. This world is not his world; this life his life.

"It's Cash and Jewel and Vardaman and Dewey Dell," pa says, kind of hangdog and proud too, with his teeth and all, even if he wouldn't look at us. "Meet Mrs Bundren," he says.

Cash -- perfect work
* thru rain
* bevel
* fill holes (82)
* takes mud off
  coffin + uses leave
  to remove stain (103)

* coffin isn't balanced
  in wagon.

* bury Addie first

WILLIAM FAULKNER, born New Albany, Mississippi, September 25, 1897—died July 6, 1962. Enlisted Royal Air Force, Canada, 1918. Attended University of Mississippi. Traveled in Europe 1925-1926. Resident of Oxford, Mississippi, where he held various jobs while trying to establish himself as a writer. First published novel, *Soldiers' Pay*, 1926. Writer in Residence at the University of Virginia 1957-1958. Awarded the Nobel Prize for Literature 1950.

AS I LAY DYING, published October 6, 1930, was Faulkner's fifth novel. The corrections in this edition are based on a collation, under the direction of James B. Meriwether, of the first edition and Faulkner's original manuscript and typescript. This volume is reproduced photographically from the corrected and reset edition published by Random House, Inc., in 1964.

* Daughter won't loan
  him $. (246)

→ can get
  the teeth.

poor man —
      such unfortunes
* sweat
* Jefferson to bury (28)
* rain storm (73)
* river is high (108)
* Beguidg her (110
* toolp   155

* Fire 209

× 223

listed on 194